THE GREEK TYCOON'S DISOBEDIENT BRIDE

D0101314

PROLOGUE

THE Greek billionaire Lysander Metaxis strode into the luxurious salon of his fabulous yacht, where his personal staff awaited him. It was half past seven in the morning. Aware that their hugely wealthy and dynamic employer usually started work at six and rarely slept more than five hours, everyone was striving to look wide awake.

His senior PA, Dmitri, presented him with a folder. 'I hope you'll be pleased, sir.'

His lean, dark, handsome face intent, Lysander withdrew the photographs of Madrigal Court. Dense woodland on all sides screened the Elizabethan manor house from curious eyes, but not from the air. His only previous acquaintance with the ancient building was through his mother's childhood photograph albums. The superb definition of the aerial shots revealed the extensive deterioration that had taken place in recent decades.

His metallic-bronze gaze grew steadily harder and colder, for it was clear that the listed building was in serious need of repair. The roof was in a mess, the brickwork required attention and there was a suspicious bulge in a gable wall. Yet, Gladys Stewart had repeatedly refused to sell the property to his late father, Aristide. However, the old lady was dying now and he could only assume that her demise would finally make the purchase of the house possible.

Madrigal Court had belonged to his mother's family for over four hundred years before financial adversity had forced its sale. Over time the reacquisition of Madrigal Court had become a matter of Metaxis family honour. And family honour was an issue that Lysander, who was Greek to his backbone, held in very high regard. His ruthlessness was legendary and he was a dangerous man to cross. But even though he was one of the richest men in the world, he had never forgotten his humble beginnings or the cruel neglect he had endured before fortune had smiled on him and given him Virginia and Aristide Metaxis as adoptive parents.

The acknowledgement of that inestimable debt spawned dark brooding thoughts, which cast disturbing shadows across Lysander's usual emotional coolness. Recent developments had made buying back Virginia's ancestral home a burning mission, as opposed to an ambition to be attained at some unspecified future date. Whatever it took he had to get the house back and quickly. All of a sudden time was of the essence, he conceded bleakly.

A stunning brunette, clad in a transparent wrap that concealed nothing of her astonishing figure, strolled in. Her caressing fingertips inscribed a provocative pattern on the back of his hand. 'Come back to bed,' she whispered invitingly.

Almost imperceptibly, Lysander stiffened. 'I'm busy,' he drawled without expression.

His staff exchanged significant glances. No woman ever held Lysander's attention for longer than a few weeks. His current lover might not know it yet, but she was already history.

'Dmitri…' Lysander lifted his well-shaped dark head '…who authorised polythene tunnels to be installed inside the walled garden?'

The PA stepped forward and frowned down at the photo in frank bewilderment. 'Er…isn't that part of Madrigal Court's grounds, sir? I'm afraid I have no idea.'

Lysander dealt Dmitri a fulminating appraisal and told him to get the Metaxis legal team on the phone for a conference call. For his UK lawyers, it became a day of unalloyed misery and grovelling apology. The rolling of heads was threatened, sacrifices were made. They promised immediate action, but the Greek tycoon commanded them to do nothing for the present. When he wanted action, he would choose the timing.

CHAPTER ONE

'The Metaxis family are waiting for me to die.' Feverish hatred burned in Gladys Stewart's embittered gaze. 'Vultures—that's what they are!'

'Well, whoever they are they'll have to wait a little longer,' the nurse informed the older woman cheerfully while she checked her blood pressure. 'You have great vitality.'

'You've got no business interrupting a private conversation!' her patient hissed in a tone of pure vitriol, her thin hands clenching on the bedclothes. 'I was addressing my granddaughter. Ophelia…where *are* you? *Ophelia?*'

A young woman with unusual pale blue eyes was engaged in piling up discarded bed linen. Directing an apologetic glance at the district nurse, she moved forward. Small in stature, she wore a loose sweater and trousers that only hinted at her hourglass figure. Hair the colour of ripe wheat was tied up with a piece of gardening twine. But nothing could hide her beauty.

'I'm here,' she told her grandmother.

As she studied her Gladys Stewart's narrow mouth compressed with furious resentment. 'If you made more effort, you'd have had a husband years ago!' she condemned bitterly.

'Your mother was a complete fool but at least she knew how to make the most of her looks!'

Ophelia, who was single by choice and inclination, thought wryly of her late parent's love affair with the mirror and almost shuddered. She liked comfy clothes and fresh air. 'Unfortunately it didn't do her much good.'

'I always swore I'd make the Metaxis family pay and I have and—listen to me—I'm not finished yet!' The claw-like hand that closed in a painful grip round Ophelia's slender wrist forced the younger woman to lean down. 'You just might have Lysander Metaxis himself knocking on this door!'

Ophelia was noticeably unimpressed by the highly unlikely forecast that a womanising billionaire, notorious for carrying the equivalent of a harem on board his giant pleasure-yacht, would ever seek her out. 'I really don't think so.'

'All you need is this house,' Gladys hissed with wheezing satisfaction in her granddaughter's ear, 'and I promise you— it'll make your every hope and dream come true.'

The fierce conviction of that final startling statement pinned Ophelia's attention squarely on her grandmother. The confusion in the younger woman's eyes was replaced by a burgeoning look of hope. 'Are you talking about…Molly?' she whispered unevenly.

Well aware that Ophelia was now hanging on her every word, Gladys turned her head away, triumph etched in every line of her bony face. 'That's for me to know and you to wonder. But if you do your duty by me and play your cards right, you won't be disappointed.'

'Finding out where my sister is *would* be everything I've ever dreamt of,' Ophelia admitted steadily. 'It would mean the world to me.'

A harsh laugh escaped the woman in the bed. 'You always were a sentimental idiot!'

A quiet knock on the door heralded the arrival of the vicar. 'Try and get some rest while you've got the chance,' the nurse urged Ophelia in an undertone.

Ophelia nodded, bundled up the bedding and gave the vicar a welcoming smile. He was a kind man, who made regular visits and met her grandmother's barrage of caustic complaints with forbearance.

'You're wasting your time,' Gladys told the reverend sourly. 'I'm not leaving a penny to that church of yours!'

Ophelia marvelled that her grandmother could still talk as though she were rich when, in fact, she was up to her ears in debt. Of course Gladys Stewart would never admit that embarrassing truth; she was obsessed with money, social position and the keeping up of appearances. Yet Madrigal Court, the moated Elizabethan manor that Gladys Stewart had persuaded her late husband to buy, was crumbling into a pitiful state of disrepair. After decades of neglect the roof was leaking, damp was spreading and most of the remaining grounds had returned to nature. Letting the beautiful old house go to rack and ruin while refusing to sell it back to the Metaxis family was part of her revenge.

From the landing window, Ophelia could see beyond the rambling gardens of the Court. Almost all the surrounding area now belonged to Lysander Metaxis, the Greek shipping magnate. His father had been wealthy, but his son and heir had the Midas touch and he had billions to burn. When it came to splashing around cash nobody could do it better than Lysander Metaxis. Every time a local property came on the market it was snapped up at a price no one else could match. Thirty-odd years ago, the only stake the Metaxis family had had in the neighbourhood was the gatehouse at the foot of the drive. Now the Metaxis estate owned most of the local farms and half the cottages in the village.

Madrigal Court was a little island of independence at the heart of a Metaxis-dominated community and very soon— for Gladys Stewart was dying—Lysander Metaxis would own the glorious old house as well. There would be no stopping him, Ophelia reflected ruefully. Even if her grandmother did leave her a share of the Court, which was by no means certain, the sheer burden of unpaid bills and death duties would ensure that the house and gardens had to be sold as soon as possible. Ophelia was hoping and praying that, when that time came, Lysander Metaxis would have no objection to her renting the walled garden for her continued use. After all, it was a good distance from the house and enjoyed a separate entrance onto the road.

Having put the bedding in the washing machine, Ophelia pulled on wellington boots and sped outdoors. She rarely managed to sleep during the day and was convinced that even twenty minutes of work in the fresh air raised her energy levels. In comparison to the rest of the grounds, which she had found impossible to maintain alone, the walled garden was an oasis of beauty and order. There, in carefully designed borders, she grew the rare perennials that she intended to make the mainstay of a small business. Although she already had a steady flow of local customers she wasn't yet in a position to hire anyone to work with her.

After half an hour of energetic digging, she made a reluctant return indoors. Discarding her boots, she padded into the atmospheric old kitchen. A range stove installed in the nineteen twenties ensured a comforting background level of warmth and remained the most modern appliance in the room.

'Good afternoon, Ophelia,' Haddock greeted her in the plummy tones at which he excelled.

'Afternoon, Haddock,' Ophelia responded.

'Time for tea, time for tea!' Haddock informed her, patrolling his perch.

Ophelia took the hint and fetched a peanut to give the parrot. She was hugely attached to him. He was almost sixty years old.

'Lovely Haddock! Lovely Haddock!' the bird opined.

Knowing his need for affection, Ophelia smoothed his feathered head and cuddled him.

Familiar footsteps sounded in the stone corridor. Pamela Arnold, a woman in her late twenties with short red hair and lively brown eyes, strolled in. 'You definitely need a man to get up close and personal with.'

'No, thanks. I'm not that desperate yet.' Ophelia wasn't joking either for, with the exception of her long-departed grandfather, the men in her life had always been a source of trouble, heartache and disillusionment. Her father had walked out when she was very young. Once he had started a new family with his second wife he had forgotten that Ophelia existed. Her mother had dated men who'd cheated her out of money, beaten her up and betrayed her with other women. And Ophelia's first love had told lies about her that had led to her being horribly bullied at school.

'Oh, no…are you feeding us again?' Ophelia groaned, embarrassed at the sight of the other woman settling a casserole dish on the scrubbed pine table. 'I can't let you keep on doing this—'

'Why not? You're run off your feet right now,' Pamela

pointed out. 'You're also my best friend and, even though I don't agree with the way you're sacrificing yourself, I need to help any way I can.'

Ophelia raised a brow in disagreement. 'I am not sacrificing myself—'

'Yes, you are, and you're doing it for a rather unpleasant person. But I'll button my disrespectful lips and say no more.'

'My grandmother helped my mother out financially and gave me a home when I needed one. She didn't have to do either of those things.' Ophelia said nothing more because Gladys Stewart's abrasive manner had always alienated people. A strong woman who had battled her passage out of poverty and defied the rigid British class system to marry a man from a superior background, Gladys had never been the type to turn the other cheek. But ultimately it had taken only one severe disappointment to poison Gladys's grim disposition beyond redemption and virtually destroy Ophelia's more fragile mother, Cathy.

Although it was more than thirty years since the day it had happened, the echoes of anger, bitterness, pain and humiliation had still contrived to leave an indelible mark on Ophelia's life. While she had struggled to keep an open mind, the people most hurt by that calamity had been those she'd loved and depended on. Naturally her family's suffering and bone-deep prejudice had had their effect on her as well. The very name Metaxis had a silent menace that filled Ophelia with a disquiet and antagonism that was foreign to her generous nature.

As Ophelia made coffee she screened a giant yawn.

As if he understood, Haddock whistled a stirring if tuneless rendering of a well-known lullaby.

Momentarily transported back in time, Ophelia tensed. Once, Haddock had sung nursery rhymes to her little sister at bedtime. The memory of Molly's beaming face below her tangle of dark curls upset Ophelia. Although she'd been only eight years old when Molly had been born, she had looked after her because their mother, Cathy, had not been up to the task. But it was now eight years since Ophelia had seen her sister.

'Shush, Haddock,' Pamela scolded, covering her ears from the din.

Offended, the parrot pointedly turned his back on the redhead.

'Haddock is a very clever parrot,' Ophelia appeased the bird in a wobbly voice.

'Haddock is a very clever parrot,' the bird repeated smugly.

'The Metaxis estate is putting up the money to repair the village community hall,' Pamela said. 'I bet it makes them more popular locally than ever.'

'Metaxis bounder—good-for-nothing swine!' Haddock screeched out at the highest decibel level, his beady eyes having fired up the instant he heard that name. 'There'll never be a Metaxis at Madrigal Court!'

An anguished groan escaped Pamela. 'Sorry, I forgot and I've set him off now.'

'Dirty rotten rascal! Makes up to one woman, runs off with another! You can't trust a Metaxis!'

'It's not Haddock's fault. People will say inappropriate things in front of him,' Ophelia complained.

'I know…I taught him sleazebag and creep because his vocabulary is getting very dated.'

'Metaxis bastard!'

'Haddock!' Ophelia gasped.

Haddock hung his head in mock shame and shuffled on his perch. Ophelia was unimpressed because, like all parrots, Haddock craved attention and loved to entertain his audience.

'Well, I didn't teach him that one,' Pamela said defensively.

Although Ophelia knew who had, she said nothing. Her way of getting through a difficult present was to stay focused on the future. She had revelled in the horticultural course she had completed at a further education college but her responsibilities at home had prevented her from pursuing an independent career. She was now twenty-five years old. The plants she grew in the walled garden had become a lifeline while she had to devote the rest of her attention to looking after a giant crumbling house and caring for a sick elderly relative. In recent times those tasks had been carried out against a stressful background of unsettled bills and an ever-dwindling income. What a shame that the billionaire Lysander Metaxis wouldn't be coming knocking on her door any time soon! She wondered what strange fancies were playing on her grandmother's mind, as the older woman had never been known for her sense of humour.

'I don't like having my time wasted,' Lysander Metaxis informed his most senior London lawyer.

'I have established that, surprising though it may seem, you *do* appear in Mrs Stewart's will as a beneficiary. I understand that your presence is crucial to the reading of the will and her solicitor has agreed to a date that will be convenient for you.'

Lysander released his breath in a slow soundless hiss. He had no time for mysteries. Why would Gladys Stewart have included him in her will? It made no sense at all.

'Possibly the lady regretted her behaviour towards your family while she was alive and this may be her way of smoothing matters over now that's she gone,' the lawyer proffered, unnerved by his most powerful client's continuing silence. 'Deathbed changes of heart are more common than you might think.'

'I don't require the woman's blessing to buy the place.' Lysander had never met Gladys Stewart. His late father, however, had once described her as a malevolent gold-digging harpy. Certainly, her ongoing hatred had caused his parents, Aristide and Virginia, a certain amount of angst over the years. Lysander had placed that at the door of his adoptive parents' overactive consciences. After all, what was the big deal? His father had only broken off his engagement to Gladys's daughter, Cathy, to marry Virginia instead. These things happened and normal people learnt to deal with them.

Forty-eight hours later, Lysander's helicopter landed at Madrigal Court. As usual, he did not travel alone. With him was a mini-posse of attentive staff and his most recent bed partner, Anichka, a six-foot-tall Russian blonde who featured on the front cover of no less than two exclusive fashion magazines that month.

'What a beautiful house,' a female aide pronounced in an unexpectedly dreamy voice.

The huge rambling manor was built of mellow brick and adorned with gracious mullioned window bays and a fantastical roofline that was a riot of tall ornate chimneys, gables and turrets. Lysander was unimpressed. History had never held much attraction for him and a dilapidated building surrounded by unkempt gardens offended his partiality for order and discipline. If so many flaws were visible at first glance, they were probably only the tip of the iceberg, Lysander thought grimly, his sensual mouth hardening. Carrying out repairs quickly would be an enormous challenge.

'It's falling apart,' Anichka remarked with distaste, brushing herself free of the rust particles that adhered to her skin when she was unwise enough to rest a hand on the wrought-iron balustrade that edged the stone bridge over the moat.

The medieval studded oak door stood ajar on a cluttered stone porch. In a critical glance Lysander took in walls in dire need of paint, gloomy, heavily carved dark panelling and shabby Victorian reproduction furniture. It was a dump, a genuine twenty-four-carat dump, on the brink of ruin. But, no matter what the price, he was going to have to buy it. Billionaire that he was, he was also a hard-hitting businessman. The prospect before him was the ultimate challenge for a male who had never before been forced to put sentiment ahead of practicality.

Morton, the solicitor, greeted Lysander in the Great Hall, suggested his party await him there and escorted him into a faded drawing room where most of the furniture was eerily shrouded in dust covers.

'Unfortunately, Mrs Stewart's granddaughter, Ophelia, has been delayed, but she should be along soon,' the older man advanced in a tone of abject apology.

At that same moment, Ophelia was ramming her ancient and battered Land Rover to a shrieking halt in the courtyard. She was running late and furious about it because even though she had told the solicitor that she had a prior arrangement for that afternoon he had ignored the information. Money talked, as the old saying went, and self-evidently a Greek billionaire was a much more important person than she was.

That attitude infuriated Ophelia because it was barely a week since her grandmother's funeral had taken place and her every free moment had been taken up with the mountain of tasks that followed bereavement. Indeed, so busy had she been that she'd had to offer a personal delivery of plants for her best customer, who had twice called at the walled garden and found her not to be there. Furthermore, the solicitor had sat on the information that Lysander Metaxis would also be attending the will reading and had only given Ophelia twenty-four-hours' notice of that extraordinary fact.

Ophelia hurried through the kitchen, thinking of what an absolute waste of time it was to have dragged Lysander Metaxis all the way to Madrigal Court. After all, for what possible reason would her grandmother have included a member of the family she had loathed in her last will and testament? Initially incredulous at Donald Morton's astonishing announcement, Ophelia had reached the uneasy conclusion that the inclusion of a Metaxis in the will could only mean that her grandmother had done something vindictive as a footnote to her departure from the world. But what exactly that might encompass Ophelia could not begin to imagine.

She accepted that Lysander Metaxis would very probably be the buyer and new owner of Madrigal Court. She even accepted that that was probably the kindest fate the ancient property could have, because it definitely did need someone with pots of money to spend. But, regardless of those facts, she would very much have preferred *not* to meet Lysander, because she could not forget that his father had totally destroyed her mother's life and, through her, that of her children. Aristide had been a playboy as well. Rich, spoilt and selfish, a womaniser, who'd never stopped to consider the damage he'd caused. And, by all accounts, Lysander Metaxis was much worse than his late father, though society was now less censorious and he could get away with a great deal more in the field of decadent living. He would be the first Metaxis to cross the threshold of Madrigal Court in over thirty years.

A baffling collection of people were waiting in the Great Hall: three men and one woman in business suits. The second woman was an incredibly lovely blonde in a brief lime-green dress. She was engaged in displaying her extremely long legs and basking like a queen in the drooling admiration of the men present.

'Good afternoon,' Ophelia said as she walked past.

Outside the drawing room door, Ophelia breathed in deep. A nervous pulse had started beating horribly fast at the foot of her throat.

Donald Morton, the family solicitor, had a harassed air and he rushed to perform introductions. 'Mr Metaxis...this is Ophelia Carter.'

'Mr Metaxis...' Ophelia's response was stilted. She froze beneath the onslaught of stunning dark eyes that had the rich shimmer of bronze. Although she had seen photos of him in newspapers she had not realised how tall he would be. He towered over her easily at six feet two inches and bore little resemblance to his short, stockily built father. Her breath caught in her tight throat, as Lysander was an astonishingly handsome man with black cropped hair and lean strong features dominated by the penetrating power of his deep-set dark gaze. The perfection of his sculpted masculine mouth was accentuated by a faint dark blue rough shadow. Even she was immediately aware of his raw sexual appeal and that shook her, for in general men left her pretty much untouched.

'Miss Carter.' Lysander had narrowed his intense gaze, for he was ensnared by something he couldn't quite define. She was tiny with a mass of blonde hair as golden as sunlight anchored to the top of her head. Her eyes were a clear crystalline blue, set in a beautiful heart-shaped face. At first he barely noticed that she was dressed like a tramp in a worn waxed jacket with her jeans tucked into muddy boots because, when she shed that jacket, her shirt revealed surprisingly full curves above and below her small waist. He decided she was hot *seriously* hot, and his sexual response was instant and painfully strong. The immediacy of that reaction startled him.

Registering that Lysander Metaxis's gaze was welded to the swell of her full breasts, Ophelia flushed pink and she lifted her chin and whispered angrily, 'What do you think you're looking at?'

Lysander could not recall a single incident when a woman had reacted with hostility to his attention, especially not one the tiny size of her, he reflected with rare amusement, reckoning that he could probably pick her up with one hand. He wondered if the impudence was deliberate and designed to enhance his interest. 'Maybe it's the boots…' he murmured, slow and soft.

An indefinable undertone in his rich dark drawl made Ophelia's entire skin surface prickle with awareness. She connected with heavily lashed bronze eyes that had the seismic effect of an earthquake on her composure. Her mouth ran dry, her heartbeat racing like a trapped bird fluttering within her ribcage.

'I like boots,' Lysander purred in lazy addition while the solicitor looked between them in growing bewilderment. 'With heels. I'm not into mud or rubber though.'

That wicked combination of mockery and suggestiveness outraged and discomfited Ophelia, who didn't know how to handle it. Her face hot enough to fry eggs on, she finally tore her eyes from him and sank down rigid-backed into an armchair, refusing to look back at him or respond.

'Let's get started,' Lysander urged the solicitor.

Ophelia discovered that she was hoping that whatever was

in the will that related to Lysander Metaxis would hammer a huge dent in his boundless self-assurance. How dared he poke fun at her appearance? He was a barefaced womaniser with a notorious reputation. Why was she allowing him to annoy her? Since when had she cared how she looked? She recalled her late mother's obsession with her appearance! Money needed for food and rent had often been squandered. All Ophelia's clothes were extremely practical.

'There are certain points I should make clear in advance,' Donald Morton said tautly. 'The will was drawn up four months ago when Mrs Stewart realised that her illness was terminal. She was determined that there should be no grounds for having the terms of the will set aside by a court. To that end she underwent a medical and psychiatric evaluation, which pronounced her fully mentally fit and able.'

Ophelia's tension grew, as it seemed obvious to her that the will was a peculiar one. She hoped she wasn't about to be embarrassed although she could imagine no circumstances in which she would apologise to a Metaxis for anything to do with her family.

'"I leave Madrigal Court and its contents in equal shares to my granddaughter, Ophelia Carter, and to Lysander Metaxis, provided that they marry—"'

'Marry?' Lysander Metaxis cut in in an abrasive tone of disbelief.

Shock welded Ophelia's slim hands to the arms of the seat. Her pale blue eyes had flown wide. 'But that's absolutely ridiculous!'

'I'm afraid that the terms of the will are unusual and challenging. Some effort was made to dissuade Mrs Stewart but the lady knew her own mind. If a marriage takes place certain conditions will have to be met for the bequest to be fulfilled. The marriage must last for a year or more and this property must also be occupied by both of you on a regular basis.'

It was the craziest list of demands that Ophelia had ever heard. *Marriage!* With their combined family history the very suggestion mortified her pride. But while the rest of the world had long since moved on, Gladys Stewart had remained stuck in the bitterness of the distant past. Evidently the will was her grandmother's last desperate attempt to gain her revenge thirty-odd years after the day that Aristide Metaxis had jilted Ophelia's mother, Cathy, at the altar.

The big society wedding of which Gladys Stewart had been so proud had turned into an instrument of family humiliation. When she'd been on the very brink of achieving her snobbish ambition of marrying her daughter off to a rich, well-connected man, it had all blown up in her face. The bridegroom had defected at the eleventh hour with the aristocratic and impoverished Virginia Waveney, who had then lived in the gatehouse at the foot of Madrigal Court's drive. Unhappily all too many people had gloried in Gladys's discomfiture, for she had never been popular, and the older woman's raging resentment had turned inward like a canker.

'Marriage is naturally not an option.' The insane suggestion that it could be gave Lysander's voice a sardonic edge of disdain.

Ophelia bridled at the soft note of silken derision that laced his accented drawl and threw her head high. 'Not if I was dragged kicking and screaming to the altar—he's a Metaxis!' she vented.

The solicitor gaped at her.

'Try to restrain your taste for melodrama until the legal niceties have been dealt with,' Lysander advised with lethal scorn.

Ophelia honestly didn't know how she managed not to stand up and thump him. Her eyes blazing as blue as a flame in the heart of a fire, she looked at him. 'I didn't like your tone of voice—'

'I'm a Metaxis and proud of it.' Shimmering bronze eyes struck sparks off hers in cold challenge. 'Keep quiet and let the grown-ups deal with business.'

Ophelia plunged upright like a jack-in-the-box on a spring. His unapologetic insolence outraged her. 'Don't you dare speak to me like that!' she launched at him.

Lysander was entertained by the ease with which she rose to the bait.

'Ophelia…Mr Metaxis…*please* let me finish,' Donald Morton interposed in a pained plea…

CHAPTER TWO

WITH colour burnishing her cheeks and silky golden strands of hair descending from her wobbly topknot, Ophelia was trembling with a rage unlike any she had ever experienced. Slowly, grudgingly, she forced herself to sit down again in the seething silence.

'If no marriage takes place, Madrigal Court will go to Ophelia's third cousin, Cedric Gilbert,' Donald Morton hastened to tell them.

'But my grandmother hated Cedric—she wouldn't even let him into the house!' Ophelia gasped.

Cedric was a wealthy property speculator. When Gladys had discovered that her husband's relative had been making sly enquiries about his chances of gaining planning permission for a housing estate at Madrigal Court, she had been outraged by his greed and calculation.

'I should add that although Mr Gilbert would inherit in those circumstances,' the solicitor continued, 'his ownership would be restricted by an agreement neither to sell the house nor try to develop the site for five years.'

The angles of Lysander's bold bronzed profile hardened. 'And if he were to break those rules?'

'The entire estate would then devolve to the government. Mrs Stewart was keen to eradicate any potential loopholes.'

Lysander, who always thought fastest in a tight corner, was engaged in suppressing a lacerating tide of fury. He could not recall when anyone had last got the better of him. That an elderly woman he had never met should have succeeded in boxing him into a corner was a lesson that some might have deemed salutary but which Lysander deemed offensive in the extreme. He wondered if Gladys Stewart had somehow discovered his position and composed her absurd will with a callous awareness of that background pressure in mind. Yet how could she have had access to confidential family information? In the time frame concerned it was impossible, he conceded harshly.

When the solicitor went on to list the substantial debts that had accrued against the estate, Ophelia grew pale since she often lay awake at night worrying about how they would be paid. The utility bills and the council tax were all outstanding and she had no idea how she would contrive to pay off her share of them, for she had nothing valuable to sell. She squirmed at the humiliation of having such personal financial business laid bare in the presence of Lysander Metaxis.

'Was there any other information…er…left for me?' Ophelia was dismayed that the will hadn't even mentioned her sister Molly's existence.

The older man peered at her over the top of his spectacles. 'Well, there is a letter to be given to you on the occasion of your wedding.'

As a wedding was most unlikely to arise, frustration and fierce disappointment flared through Ophelia. As quickly she scolded herself for assuming that the letter might contain anything that would help her to track down her sister. After all, if the tenor of her grandmother's will revealed anything, it was that Gladys Stewart's overweening desire for revenge had meant infinitely more to her than family ties. How *could* her grandmother have made such a preposterous demand in her will? Two strangers marrying to inherit a house? As if Lysander Metaxis would be desperate enough to go to those lengths to acquire Madrigal Court!

Lysander brought the meeting to a swift conclusion.

'I would be grateful if you could both confirm your final intentions with regard to the will within the week,' the solicitor remarked in an apologetic tone.

Lysander Metaxis rose lithely from his seat. 'Ophelia? I want a tour of the house.'

Unprepared for that declaration, Ophelia bristled. Where the heck did he get the nerve to demand a tour after the way he had spoken to her? And he *was* demanding, for that blunt statement was light years away from a polite request. Then maybe he didn't know *how* to be polite. Maybe he was just a bone-deep arrogant boor with no concept of good manners. That idea soothed her temper.

'I'm sorry, no, it's not convenient,' Ophelia breathed curtly, blanking the tall powerful Greek while catching sight of the solicitor's dismay at her refusal. But Lysander Metaxis inspired her with sheer loathing and she saw no reason to pretend otherwise. After all, they lived in different worlds and would never meet again in this lifetime.

'I never ask for favours. You give me the official tour and I'll pay your water charges,' Lysander drawled smooth as glass.

Ophelia could barely believe that he had made such a de-grading offer. As if her tolerance and time could be purchased with his wretched money! On the other hand, it was a very generous offer and could she really afford to turn it down? Why shouldn't he have to pay? It was a real climb-down after his rudeness, a victory really, Ophelia's agile brain reasoned. Letting him pay was like fining him for bad behaviour and it was perfectly possible that he only appreciated what he had to pay for.

'*All* of the water charges?' Ophelia enquired stiffly, angrily rejecting the inner reflection that two wrongs did not make a right.

'Ophelia…I really don't think—' Donald Morton, engaged in tidying up his papers at the table, was aghast at the dialogue.

'Ophelia and I understand each other very well,' Lysander interposed silkily. 'All the water charges.'

'I want the money now—cash up front,' Ophelia told him.

A reluctant glitter of appreciation brightened his dark deep-set eyes. 'I want to see the bill.'

'It's not a problem, Mr Metaxis,' Ophelia declared in a honeyed voice as if his every wish were now her command.

Satisfied that for the right price Ophelia Carter would do as she was told, Lysander repaired to the hall and unfurled his mobile phone to ring his lawyers. He spared a brief thought to the character of the late Gladys Stewart, whose determination to extract revenge from beyond the grave had made her choose to die in poverty rather than sell up. A lady with a gothic taste for retribution, Lysander conceded in harsh acknowledgement. While he was still on the phone, Anichka wandered in and wound her lithe body round him. Irritation slivered through him, since he liked his own space in bed *and* out of bed.

But the powerful rage was now contained and cooled inside

him. Lysander never let his emotions take control. Within seconds of a challenge he was working out how to turn the tables and win. He never accepted defeat and he knew that success always came at a cost. In short, he could see no way out of marrying Ophelia Carter. It was a preposterous demand, but what other option did he have in the short term? A delay of five years was out of the question. Challenging the will in court would take too long and there would be no guarantee of success. He would also have to own the house to restore it to a presentable level.

As for Ophelia, she was facing a stack of debts and she was clearly as greedy as every other woman he had ever met—and a great deal more open about it than most. She would marry him, all right. Had she known what was in the will? Had she and her grandmother conspired together? Before he was finished with her, he would find out. He wondered what she would be like in bed and accepted without question that he would soon be finding that out too. Would her glowing energy and hair-trigger temper translate into passion? Country weekends, which had always been too slow and sedate for Lysander's urban spirit, were suddenly beginning to offer the tantalising promise of sexual compensation.

Ophelia took the service stairs down to the basement two at a time. Obviously Cedric was going to inherit Madrigal Court. Her grandmother must have known that that would be the result of such a facetious will, Ophelia acknowledged wryly. But then Gladys had always preferred men to women and had often lamented her lack of a male heir. Ophelia found Pamela waiting for her in the kitchen.

'*Well?*' Pamela gasped in excitement. 'Is Lysander as fanciable in the flesh as he looks in celebrity magazines?'

'Lysander has all the winsome charm of a rattlesnake.' Ophelia avoided using the surname that set off Haddock's fiercest outbursts.

'Ly…san…der,' Haddock mimicked, for he loved new words.

Ophelia was keen to avoid a repetition that would encourage the parrot and she ignored him while she rifled through the old desk in the far corner.

'What are you looking for?' Pamela queried in wonderment. 'What about the will?'

'I haven't got time to tell you, but it's not good. Anyway, I've agreed to give Lysander Metaxis a full tour of the house.'

'Why on earth have you agreed to do that?'

'Because he's paying the water charges…' As her friend regarded her with a literal dropped jaw Ophelia shrugged a defensive shoulder and hauled off her boots. 'Well, he's a smart-ass and he offered to pay them just to embarrass me and underline the fact that I'm poor and he's filthy rich. I was so furious I just said yes. Why not?'

'Why not…' Pamela was too taken aback to respond further.

Ophelia pelted back upstairs in her woolly boot socks. In the outer hall she was jolted by the sight of Lysander's flamboyant blonde girlfriend leaning up against him, her full lips pouting, her expression one of avidity. Her hands were splayed across his chest, her pelvis angled into his big powerful frame with a blatant eroticism that made Ophelia feel grossly uncomfortable. For an awful instant she found it almost impossible to look away because she had never before seen a woman look at a man with open hunger.

But Lysander was impervious to the Russian model, his brilliant gaze winging straight to Ophelia and lingering. Her eyes were vivid flashes of ice blue against the luminous perfection of her skin. Her hair was a mess, her clothes a joke, but somehow she still contrived to look spectacular. Nor could the workmanlike shirt and jeans conceal the voluptuous swell of her high breasts or the extremely feminine curve of her hips. That she was fresh from working in what would be *his* walled garden added a piquant note to his reaction.

The sudden ferocious tension in the room engulfed Ophelia and she frowned in confusion. She could feel the Greek tycoon's gaze flaring over her like flames dancing across her unprotected skin. A kernel of heat burned deep down inside her, making her conscious of her body in a way that unnerved her. Her cheeks warmed and she glanced hurriedly at his companion only to register that the other woman was subjecting her to a murderous glare.

Lysander was already setting the blonde back from him. 'Anichka, run along… I want to speak to Miss Carter in private.'

As the blonde stalked out Ophelia drew in a steadying breath. She was discovering that she didn't have to like Lysander Metaxis to find being left alone with him exciting.

'Is that the water bill?' Lysander indicated the crumpled paper clutched in her hand. 'I don't need to see it. I was joking.'

He handed her a thick wad of high-denomination banknotes and, for a split second, Ophelia didn't know what the money was for until she realised that it was the cash to settle the utility charge. She paled and almost lost her composure, because now that she had calmed down she knew that she shouldn't be accepting money from him. It was totally wrong but she couldn't think of any immediate way of giving it back that would not make her look foolish. Shamefaced, she dug the notes hurriedly into her back pocket. She would sort it out later.

Lysander shifted a shapely brown hand in a fluid gesture

that invited Ophelia to proceed. Once she had guided private tour groups round the rambling house, but the lack of facilities and safeguards for visitors had soon brought that sideline to an end. She felt horribly hollow as she realised that she could no longer regard the manor as her home.

Tense as a bowstring, Ophelia came to a halt at the foot of the stairs. 'The carving on the staircase dates to—'

'Spare me the tourist commentary,' Lysander Metaxis urged in immediate interruption. 'Show me the highlights.'

Ophelia was appalled that he could parade his lack of interest without shame. She shot him a censorious glance and it was a mistake. Her attention welded to his square masculine jaw, shifted inexorably upward to scan his wide passionate mouth and climbed without her conscious volition to take in his high carved cheekbones and the black density of his thick lashes. Disapproval was forgotten while her tummy flipped and her skin prickled. His thick dark lashes lifted: eyes the colour of molten bronze gazed steadily back at her and her throat was so constricted she honestly thought she might choke.

Tearing her attention from him, she mounted the stairs at speed, adrenalin pumping through her. 'This is the Long Gallery.'

Lysander drew level and stared down the dusty empty length of what had once been Madrigal Court's crowning glory. The curtains were ragged and the family portraits and stately furniture had long since been sold. The emptiness was not a concern because Lysander had had a team working to trace and buy back those missing heirlooms for some years. He studied the elaborate ceiling and the ancient creaking floor, which were discoloured by damp. Although his expressive mouth compressed he made no comment.

'Be careful where you walk. The floor's a little dodgy in places,' Ophelia warned.

'You seemed shocked by the will,' Lysander remarked without inflection.

'Who wouldn't have been? I'm afraid my grandmother was a law unto herself and she loved keeping secrets.' Ophelia saw no point in discussing the will with him. As far as she was concerned he had had no business appearing in it and she was not sorry that his inclusion should have proved a disappointment to him. She didn't trust herself to look directly at him. It shook her and it shamed her that she could be so powerfully attracted to a man whose lover awaited him downstairs. But then her brain seemed to play no part in the effect he had on her, she conceded guiltily. Indeed her body was alight with a crazy sort of fizzing awareness that kept on interfering with her common sense.

'As you must already be aware, I'm very keen to acquire this house,' Lysander imparted levelly.

Ophelia pressed open the door at the foot of the gallery. 'You're a rich man. I'm sure Cedric will sell it to you as soon as he's able.'

His lean, strong face hardened. 'I'm not prepared to wait five years.'

'I'm afraid you don't have a choice.' Ophelia thought it would do him no harm whatsoever to have to wait for what he wanted. He would also have to make it worth Cedric's while to ditch his development plans. Her cousin was an excessively greedy man who would be quick to take advantage of the chance to increase the worth of his unexpected inheritance. But then what possible hope did that give her of renting the walled garden from Cedric? Her heart sank at that obvious truth.

'But we *do* have a choice,' Lysander Metaxis pronounced at the precise moment that he put his foot through a rotten floorboard. With a sibilant Greek curse, he pulled free of the splintering wood and stepped back.

'I did warn you. I do wish you'd be more careful!' Ophelia groaned. 'There are loads of holes on the floor above but until now I've been able to keep this floor pretty much intact.'

Recognising criticism rather than concern and apology in those comments, Lysander was torn between anger and astonishment. 'I could've been hurt.'

'I doubt that you're that fragile, but below this room is an irreplaceable ceiling that is almost five hundred years old,' Ophelia told him waspishly.

She showed him a selection of panelled bedrooms and the shabby main reception rooms on the ground floor. Lysander disliked everything he saw: the disrepair and dinginess, the ponderous Victorian furniture and the faded tatters of long-departed grandeur. When she suggested taking him outdoors to show him the grounds, he demurred and directed her back into the drawing room instead.

'We have to discuss the will.' Lysander had one goal: to win her immediate agreement to meet the terms and get back to London without any further expenditure of his valuable time and energy. 'I want this house and, although it is not my way to surrender to virtual blackmail, I'm prepared to marry you to get it.'

Ophelia was stunned by that admission and stared back at him with wide eyes. It had not once occurred to her that a male as wealthy and influential as Lysander Metaxis would be prepared to marry a stranger to get his hands on a property. After all, a simple wait of five years would allow him to acquire it by purchase. 'You can't possibly want Madrigal Court *that* much…you can't be serious!'

'Of course I am serious,' Lysander responded drily.

Ophelia shook her head in bewilderment. The movement was too much for her loose topknot and as her hair began to fall down round her in earnest she yanked out the clip and finger-combed it impatiently back from her smooth brow. 'But that doesn't make sense at all.'

Lysander watched with male sensual intensity as the heavy gold strands of her hair tumbled down and slid in silky loops across her narrow shoulders. 'It makes sense to me.'

Conscious of his appraisal but carefully avoiding it, Ophelia walked over to the window and spun restively round again. Nothing he had so far said made sense to her. 'But you could wait for Cedric to sell it to you, or maybe work out some compromise with the lawyers. If you're rich aren't there always ways and means? Why are you in such a hurry? I know that your mother's family owned this place for centuries but you've shown no real interest in the history of the house. Does the family connection really mean that much to you?'

With hauteur, Lysander elevated a sleek ebony brow. 'I have my reasons and they are private.'

Royally snubbed, Ophelia reddened. 'Yes, but to suggest that we marry as if it means nothing—'

'Essentially, it would mean nothing. All that would be required of us would be a quiet civil ceremony,' Lysander interposed. 'It's the easiest and most practical way for me to obtain Madrigal Court. The building is already in poor condition. Do you think it can wait five years for attention? I would immediately engage a team of architects and craftsmen to restore it.'

Ophelia was struggling to suppress a growing sense of indignation that he could *dare* to suggest that she marry him so that he could get his hands on the house sooner. Didn't he have any sensitivity at all? Ophelia had been raised with the sad story of how her mother had felt on the day that Aristide Metaxis stood her up at the altar. When Cathy had had a drink or two, she had talked endlessly about her broken heart. Ophelia's mother might have married another man but Aristide Metaxis had been the love of her life. Her parent's inability to overcome her feelings for Aristide and resist the temptation he offered had ultimately destroyed her and every relationship that had followed.

'There's no point talking about this because I'm not prepared to consider any form of marriage, civil or otherwise,' Ophelia declared in a flat tone of finality.

Lysander looked steadily back at her, lush black lashes semi-screening cool metallic eyes of enquiry. 'Why not?'

'It would be inappropriate.' Ophelia was determined to retain her dignity rather than descend into the kind of emotionalism that she knew would only rouse his contempt. Shame wasn't fashionable. No doubt he saw no reason why he should feel the slightest bit guilty about his father's mistreatment of her mother. 'I couldn't do it.'

'I'm sure you could.' His dark imperious features had a sardonic cast. 'The financial rewards for doing as I ask will be handsome.'

All Ophelia's natural colour drained from her complexion. The wad of banknotes in her back pocket felt as if it were burning into her flesh. 'I suppose it's my own fault that I'm getting that offer.' She hauled out the cash he had given her and settled it down with a decisive slap on the table beside her. 'Take your money back, keep it. If I hadn't been trying to outface you earlier I wouldn't have accepted it. I may be broke but I still know the difference between right and wrong.'

Lysander gave her a wolfish smile of dark amusement. 'You sound like a little girl.'

Crystalline blue eyes flaring, Ophelia lifted her chin. 'Look, it may sound stupid and simplistic to you but that's how I try to live my life. All right, I don't always live up to my own ideals, but when I make a mistake I'm not ashamed to admit it!'

'Ideals are wonderful when you can afford them.' Striking bronze eyes mocked her stance in a way that only whipped her antagonism higher. 'But if I walk away, you won't get a share of the house and you'll be in debt. Agree to my conditions and money won't be a problem for you ever again. I am generous towards those who please me.'

Her change of tune from greed to idealism left Lysander cold. He was convinced that her show of reluctance was squarely aimed at driving his price for her compliance higher. After all, she had taken the money for the water charges without hesitation: she had *wanted* the money and had seen no reason why she should not accept it. That had told Lysander all he needed to know.

His refusal to accept a negative response sent temper roaring up inside Ophelia like a geyser. 'Unfortunately for you, I haven't got the smallest desire to please you!'

His veiled gaze gleaming, Lysander vented a husky laugh of disagreement. 'I think we both know that I could persuade you otherwise with very little effort.'

Although Ophelia was furious with him and mortified that he had noticed her reaction to him, that low-pitched sonorous laugh still made her backbone tingle. Even his insolence had a curious sexual power, but it also stung her ferocious pride like acid and intensified her anger. 'No, you couldn't, and the number one reason why not is that I don't like what you are! In any case marriage is not something I could ever take lightly or use for my own ends—'

'Whether you like what I am or not should have no bearing on your decision,' Lysander countered very drily. 'Use your intelligence. At its most basic the marriage would be a convenient business arrangement of mutual benefit. You need money and I want this house sooner rather than later.'

'But I don't want to play my grandmother's games, or yours, and I genuinely don't want your money!' Ophelia retorted with an angry distaste that she couldn't hide. 'You can't bribe me into doing what you want. All right, so I'll spend a long time paying off those bills, but at the end of it I'll still be able to hold my head high because, unlike you, *I* have principles.'

Lysander had not moved a muscle. His lean bronzed features were unrevealing but the temperature in the atmosphere was steadily dropping to freezing point. 'I don't accept insults.'

'I'm not insulting you. I'm only pointing out that you appear to have no scruples,' Ophelia argued vehemently. 'What you want will always come first with you. Then you're a Metaxis, so I shouldn't be surprised.'

'I am proud of that heritage. That appears to offend you.' Granite-hard bronze eyes challenged her.

The chill in the air and the stillness of his stance were intimidating. Her heart gave a heavy thud inside her. He was tough and immovable, not at all like his lightweight charmer of a father. That stray thought roused other dim and unsettling memories and stiffened Ophelia's backbone. Why should she allow herself to be manipulated by her grandmother's will, or by Lysander Metaxis? She had been a loyal granddaughter but now it was time to reclaim her life and liberty.

'We've got nothing more to say to each other,' she pronounced, walking to the door and pulling it open in an invitation for him to leave.

'I don't like being messed around,' Lysander murmured with chilling bite.

'You just don't like the word no,' Ophelia contradicted, for she was pretty much convinced that he didn't hear that word half as much as he needed to hear it.

'You are also prejudiced against my family.'

His perception made Ophelia turn pink with chagrin. 'A little…sorry, I can't help it.'

'How can you allow something that occurred thirty years ago to influence us in the present? What took place then is not our concern.'

Furious that she had allowed him an opening to talk down to her as though he alone were the sane voice of reason, Ophelia sealed her lips on a fiery flood of disagreement. Perhaps he preferred to pretend that his father had had no further contact with her mother after he had jilted her. Or perhaps he genuinely did not know that her mother had been his father's occasional mistress for more years than Ophelia cared to recall. Whatever, Ophelia had no desire to discuss that shameful reality.

Lysander lifted a lean brown hand and tucked a business card into the breast pocket of her shirt with a sardonic cool that made her tummy muscles clench. 'My private number. But I warn you now—you've wasted my time and I won't offer you as good a deal.'

'I'm *not* going to phone you!' Ophelia launched up at him. 'Why can't you take no for an answer?'

Stunning bronzed eyes glittering, Lysander stared down at her with brooding mesmeric force. 'You'll come to me,' he forecast soft and low.

Ophelia had stopped breathing. Her entire skin surface felt cold and then hot. As he strode down the passageway she folded her arms in a jerky motion. *No way,* she wanted to scream in his wake, *no way will I ever come to you!* But the disturbing unfamiliarity of her suppressed rage shook her so much that she didn't trust herself to make any response. In the aftermath, listening to the helicopter take off noisily, she discovered that she was so tense that her muscles were literally hurting her. She had never been so angry, hadn't even known that she could get that angry. Until Lysander Metaxis came along she had always considered herself to be a quite laid-back and tolerant sort of a person.

An hour later, she drove down the long drive to the gatehouse that Pamela rented from the Metaxis estate. Her friend was in the kitchen cooking up a storm as befitted a private caterer, much in demand for her dinner-party prowess. Her nerves still jangling like piano wires that had been brutally yanked, Ophelia told the redhead what had happened.

Pamela hung on Ophelia's every word, while her brown eyes grew rounder and rounder with amazement. 'My word, why would a billionaire be *that* desperate to get his hands on Madrigal Court?'

'I don't know and I don't care.'

'Maybe he's had a geological survey done and there's a vein of gold or oil or something under the grounds. Well, why not?' Pamela demanded when Ophelia shot her a look of disbelief. 'I mean, I saw a couple of guys doing some sort of a survey in the field next door to the walled garden last month and I think they went in—'

'You saw surveyors in the walled garden and you didn't tell me?' Ophelia gasped in horror.

'I assumed they were working for the Metaxis estate and were probably just being nosy—I didn't think you needed the aggravation just then,' her friend protested.

'Sorry.' Ophelia sighed. 'I'm all strung up.'

'Of course, you're absolutely right about standing up for your principles,' Pamela remarked gingerly. 'A shame, though, because you could have settled the bills from your share of the house sale. The money would have been so useful. You could have hired a private investigator to track down your sister. I bet there'd have been enough to get your business up and running in the walled garden as well.'

Halfway through her friend's speech, Ophelia had begun deflating like a pricked balloon. *Molly!* Why on earth hadn't it occurred to her that her sister was also entitled to a share of Madrigal Court? That any decision she made now would impact on her sister's prospects as well? Sadly, Gladys Stewart had always had a different attitude to Molly, who had been born illegitimate.

When Ophelia had been sixteen years old, her mother had died in a train crash and Gladys had flown up to the girls' home in Scotland to take charge. Two days after the older woman had brought her granddaughters home to Madrigal Court, Ophelia had returned from her new school to discover that her little sister and her belongings were gone. Ophelia had been distraught but her grandmother had been unsympathetic.

'Molly's father came to collect her. He'll be looking after her from now on,' Gladys declared. 'That's how it should be.'

Stunned by that announcement, Ophelia gasped. 'But how did her father find her here? I don't even know who Molly's father is! Mum would never talk about him—'

'Molly doesn't belong here with us and you'll have to accept that. She's not your responsibility any more, she's her father's.'

Ophelia would never forget the pain of that sudden cruel separation from the little girl she had adored from birth. At first she had assumed that she would be able to stay in touch with Molly through letters and visits. When there had been no contact her grandmother had simply shrugged and insisted that she had no further information to offer. Ophelia, however, had long been convinced that there was more to the story than she was being told.

But now Ophelia had to deal with the reality that if she turned her back on her inheritance, Molly would lose out as well. When she finally found her sister, how would Molly feel about that decision? Molly was only seventeen years old. Would Molly forgive Ophelia for putting family pride and principles ahead of the chance of a substantial legacy?

'Possibly I've been a little hasty in turning down Lysander's offer,' Ophelia muttered heavily. 'But that's his fault—he made me so angry I couldn't think straight!'

Pride made Ophelia baulk at an immediate climb-down, which she felt would make her seem like the sort of woman who couldn't make up her mind and keep it for five minutes. The prospect of agreeing to a marriage of convenience with a guy she totally loathed, hated and despised also disturbed her sleep that night. It was frustrating to discover, then, that the phone number he had given her only led to a super-protective aide and not, as she had naively assumed, to the man himself. She learned that Lysander was abroad and was offered an appointment in London the following week.

Left to stew in her own juice, Ophelia became increasingly curious about the contents of the letter her grandmother had set aside for delivery on her wedding day. That mysterious letter seemed as peculiar a piece of work as the will for the unsentimental older woman. What could possibly be in it? Ophelia tried to recall her late grandparent's cryptic remarks about the house and her sister.

Gladys had brought Lysander Metaxis to Madrigal Court by naming him in her will, knowing how keen he was to regain the house. Her grandmother had also declared that Madrigal Court could make Ophelia's every hope come true. Could that mean that if Ophelia did as she was told in the will and married Lysander Metaxis, might some information about Molly's whereabouts be delivered in that letter as a reward? All of a sudden, Ophelia had a much stronger motivation for agreeing to the marriage.

What would it cost her? A meaningless link with a man she despised which would soon be severed again. She refused to think of it in terms of actual marriage, for it would not be a marriage in *any* real sense. Moreover, she had no doubt that Lysander would continue to exercise his evidently overactive libido below the roof of Madrigal Court. She grimaced at the prospect of a parade of predatory beauties wandering about her home at all hours of the day and night. They would no doubt all cling brainlessly to Lysander like burrs and behave in sexually provocative ways that embarrassed her. She winced in distaste and reminded herself that her bedroom was in the rear wing and she could doubtless stay outdoors or out of sight most of the time that he was around.

That same day Ophelia's gloomy ruminations were interrupted by an unexpected phone call from the solicitor, Donald Morton, who asked her to come and see him at his office. There he explained that he had received a visit from one of Lysander Metaxis's lawyers, along with a formal request for her to cease her use of the walled garden.

Ophelia studied the older man in utter bewilderment. 'I don't understand…'

'It has been brought to my attention that twelve years ago your grandfather sold the walled garden and the three fields beside it to a local farmer. Your grandmother appears not to have appreciated that the walled garden was included in the sale.'

Twelve years earlier, Ophelia hadn't even been living at Madrigal Court because her mother had still been alive. 'Of course, I knew that those fields were sold off ages ago…but the walled garden *can't* have been sold with them.'

'I didn't handle the sale, but I have copies of the documents here and I can assure you that it was part of the parcel.' The solicitor explained that the farmer's son had intended to open a market-gardening business, but when he had died unexpectedly the walled garden had been left undisturbed because his father had had no use for it.

Ophelia listened in mounting consternation. The Metaxis estate had bought out the farmer four years earlier and had somehow overlooked the fact that the walled garden formed part of the acquisition.

She honestly felt as though she had had a giant rock dropped on her from on high. 'You're telling me that I've been trespassing on someone else's land for almost five years? That Lysander Metaxis legally owns *my* garden?'

'And anything you have built within those walls.'

Pale as milk, Ophelia nodded like a marionette, while the solicitor expressed his sympathy for her position while advising her that there was nothing whatsoever she could do about it.

In a daze Ophelia drove straight to the walled garden, or at least she *tried*. The Metaxis estate installed swanky green farm gates at all the entrances onto their land. Such a gate was already in the process of being erected at the foot of the lane that led up to the walled garden. She drove past the workmen and leapt out of her vehicle outside the mellow brick walls that surrounded the nursery. She was shocked to see that the tall wrought-iron gates were now padlocked shut, barring her from the garden that was the living result of years of her dreams and her work.

As she boiled with rage Ophelia thought darkly, If I marry Lysander Metaxis, I will surely kill him for doing this to me! Because not for a moment did she doubt the identity of the culprit responsible for dividing her from her beloved plants…

CHAPTER THREE

THE same day that Ophelia refused to entertain his marriage proposition, Lysander began assembling a line-up of professionals to take charge of the speedy restoration of Madrigal Court.

He had no doubt that, given sufficient incentive and reward, Ophelia would cave in to his demands. Having her advised that she was trespassing on his property in utilising the walled garden was in the nature of a gentle warning shot across her bow. He wanted her to appreciate that, without his support, life could get very difficult and he was fully convinced that once he started picking up her bills she would never dirty her hands in a garden again.

Not a man to stand still or waste time, he instructed his legal team to draw up a pre-nuptial agreement and investigate ways and means of holding the ultimate in discreet weddings. When he was informed that Ophelia had requested an appointment with him, it was not a surprise. But, by then, he was in Athens and he had rather more pressing priorities to deal with.

Even in Greece, however, Lysander devoted every spare moment to business. Work and lots of it had always been his solution to problems or worries. The instant a negative thought hit him or, indeed, anything threatened to demand an emotional response, Lysander buried himself in even more work and exhausted his staff. When his employees in London had begun falling asleep on him a month earlier, he had drafted in more from Greece and suggested they work shifts to keep up with him. The day he returned to London, he pulled off a megamillion-pound deal that made headlines in all the financial pages of the newspapers, but he chose to party alone and had a diamond necklace delivered to Anichka as a goodbye gift.

The rural life had never been to his taste, but the prospect of weekends in the country with Ophelia was steadily beginning to acquire an aura of darkly erotic, forbidden appeal. Although his intelligence continually pointed out that Ophelia wasn't his type—she was too argumentative, too little and too scruffy—he had got bored with Anichka in only two weeks and suspected that his turnover rate in the bedroom was becoming excessive. A change in feminine style and tempo would revitalise him, Lysander reasoned with satisfaction. He pictured Ophelia transformed into a radiant beauty, polished to perfection and spread across a four-poster bed wearing only a welcoming smile, and his libido reacted like a Formula One car at the starting line.

When he remembered the decrepit bedstead with the tatty drapes he had seen at Madrigal Court, the fantasy almost crashed. He contacted his household team, who took care of all his properties, and voiced his first ever personal request with regard to furniture. He ordered a four-poster bed complete with hangings. It would make a terrific wedding present.

Ophelia hurried into the lift in the Metaxis building.

Getting to London in time for her appointment had necessitated a pre-dawn departure on the train. She was dressed in her best—a black wool jacket and a neat grey knee-length skirt—a stalwart outfit that she dutifully dragged out for church, funerals and all such serious occasions. She was thinking that she had never been very good at eating humble pie and she knew that Lysander Metaxis would make a three-course meal out of her capitulation. Unhappily her surrender was eating her alive from inside out, because he had dared to do the unthinkable—he had locked her out of her garden! All-out war would have felt much more natural to her.

Only Ophelia knew what her garden meant to her because she had laboured to create it from scratch. Each plant, shrub and tree had been watched over and lovingly nurtured by her. Gladys Stewart had been a cold guardian for a warm-hearted teenage girl grieving over her mother's death and the loss of her sister. Ophelia had found solace working outdoors and watching the change of the seasons, while she'd reached the conclusion that plants could be more reliable and rewarding than people.

Ophelia felt like a fish out of water in the Metaxis building, which buzzed with rushing staff and big-business energy. The huge office block was full of metal surfaces, towering pillars and glass in unexpected places. The amount of attention she got at the mere mention of Lysander's name amazed her. She was delivered straight into his large and imposing office like a parcel. He was talking on the phone in French, his bold profile silhouetted against the light. In a charcoal-grey pin-stripe suit with the faultless cut of superb tailoring, he looked staggeringly handsome. The instant that thought assailed her she wanted to punish herself for having it.

Lysander tossed down the phone and focused on Ophelia with thickly lashed metallic-bronze eyes that went from an appreciative glow to the steady coolness of ice-water. The beauty of her shining golden hair, clear light blue gaze and glowing complexion was exceptional. But the dull, dated outfit she wore was a horror and he was annoyed that she had not made more effort on the grooming front.

'Your intransigence has cost this venture a week,' he drawled grimly, his lean, strong face hard.

Still at the far end of the large office, Ophelia strove to be level-headed and practise restraint in the face of that immediate rebuke. 'It wasn't intransigence…I needed time to think your proposition over.'

'*Right,*' Lysander retaliated with the kind of stinging disbelief that could only infuriate.

Colour winging an arc across her cheekbones, Ophelia sucked in a steadying gulp of sustaining oxygen. Unfortunately it only made her feel angrier than ever, particularly when he did not immediately offer her a seat. Striving for an air of composure, she approached some sofas that were arranged in a stylish semicircle by the tall windows and sat down without invitation. 'I've decided that I'm willing to go through with the marriage plan,' she announced with dignity.

'So we are now in agreement?'

Her blue eyes glinted with the hidden fire of opals. 'As much in agreement as we're ever likely to be.'

'If you're not prepared to put your whole heart in this venture I won't go through with it.'

Surprise and dismay attacked Ophelia at that unexpected response.

'I have to be able to trust you,' Lysander pointed out. 'This won't work otherwise.'

Although Ophelia had promised herself that she would not

mention the garden until the very end of the interview, that statement broke through her self-control. 'Considering that you've locked me out of my garden, trust would be quite a challenge!'

Level bronze eyes met her angry ones.

A rebellious little frisson of sexual awareness knotted low in her pelvis. Her breasts stirred, the tender pink tips tightening inside a bra that now felt uncomfortably tight. Her heart was beating very fast. She couldn't credit how he could have that effect on her even when she was annoyed with him! Her colour heightened while she blamed her lack of experience with men on her embarrassing level of susceptibility.

'I've locked you out of *my* garden,' Lysander contradicted without a shade of discomfiture. 'But it'll be unlocked as soon as we finish hammering out the details of our arrangement.'

Her teeth gritted as she swallowed back a hostile response. It was the truth, even if she didn't like it. He owned her garden. She tried to be mollified by his assurance that the padlock would be removed once everything was settled between them. But nothing could soothe the demeaning sting of being forced to toe the line against her will and rewarded for her surrender with something she had always considered to be very much her own and which had cost him nothing.

'What kind of details?' she questioned tightly.

'You will have to sign a pre-nuptial contract.'

'All right.' Ophelia was unsurprised that his first concern was the protection of his massive wealth. 'What else?'

'To minimise the impact on our lives, I want our arrangement to remain a secret. The only people who need to be in on this are our lawyers. Have you discussed this with anyone else?'

Ophelia thought of Pamela and crossed her fingers behind her handbag and decided to fib. 'No,' she said.

'I'm applying for a special licence to speed the process up. My legal team think that St Mary's church on the edge of the Madrigal Court estate would be the most suitable location. I understand it's still in occasional use and very private.'

Ophelia was taken aback by that suggestion. 'Yes, it is. But I would honestly prefer a civil ceremony.'

'It would be virtually impossible to stage a discreet wedding in an urban register office. Although I take every possible precaution to protect my privacy, my movements do attract a great deal of publicity. I'm keen to keep the press in the dark as regards our association.' His rich dark accented drawl carried a pronounced note of finality.

Ophelia linked her slender hands together and studied them with fixed attention. Her ideas and opinions were not required. Everything was to be based on his needs and preferences, not hers, and he had already made up his mind. It wasn't the details that were being hammered out, it was her place in his scheme and he was determined to keep their future marital status a deep dark secret. Ought she to be offended by that or relieved?

'Although there won't be guests as such, we'll make the wedding as normal an occasion as possible in case the validity of the marriage is questioned at some later stage,' Lysander continued.

'Let's forget the use of that misleading word "we" when I'm not allowed to have any input,' Ophelia suggested dulcetly. 'You know you'd be much happier telling it like it is.'

Lysander studied her with hard dark eyes across the divide of the coffee-table. Her crystalline gaze was screened, her full pink mouth at a slight pout. He was not deceived by this modest look, though his attention did linger on the ripe curve of her lips. He was wondering how she could put out such a sexual vibe when she wore neither make-up nor provocative clothing. 'As you wish. You will dress like a bride for the ceremony and a photographer will record the occasion.'

'How will the living arrangements work?' she prompted tautly.

'Easily. I'll spend several days a month at Madrigal Court—generally weekends.'

'I don't think you'll be very comfortable there.' Ophelia was trying without success to imagine him taking up residence in a house that was full of history and charm but very short on luxury and convenience.

'My household staff will take whatever measures are necessary to ensure my comfort and yours,' Lysander declared. 'Everything will be organised in advance.'

Ophelia dared to look up and, encountering his stunning metallic eyes, felt as if she had been zapped by an electric current that set every nerve and skin cell jangling. In haste she tore her attention from him and got up to wander restively round the room. 'How long do you think we'll have to keep up the pretence?'

'Fourteen months at most,' he told her, letting her know that the matter had been considered with care and reduced to as short a period as would be deemed acceptable in the circumstances. 'But I must warn you that if word of the marriage leaks into the public domain, everything will change and we'll have to pretend that it's for real. Is that understood?'

'Yes, of course,' Ophelia agreed without really thinking about that possibility. 'But in the meantime I just go on as if I'm still Ophelia Carter, rather than your wife.'

'I may not want you to behave like a wife,' Lysander hastened to assure her with sardonic immediacy, 'but you *will* have to behave as though you're in a relationship with me.'

Ophelia shot him a startled glance. 'In a relationship?' she echoed in bemusement. 'I hope you're joking—'

'Why would we be going through this whole charade just to blow it by acting like strangers when we're beneath the same roof?' Lysander demanded with lancing impatience. 'That is out of the question—'

'But you'll still have your…er…women, won't you?' Ophelia cut in thinly, both tone and lips compressed.

'Not at Madrigal Court. In the light of authenticity, you will be the only woman in that household.'

Ophelia was interested to note that he did have some boundaries and relieved that she was not going to be expected to deal with his womanising activities and carousing on the doorstep, as it were. A split second later, however, she recalled the original argument and angry discomfiture gripped her. 'But if people don't appreciate that we're married…for goodness' sake, what are they going to think I am?'

'My housekeeper who sleeps with me, an occasional lover, whatever.' Lysander shrugged with magnificent disregard on the score of what her feelings might be. 'Nobody is likely to rate the connection any higher if I never take you out of the house, and the more casual it seems, the less interest it generates. What does it matter?'

Outrage was roaring through Ophelia in an enervating surge. 'It matters a heck of a lot to me! A housekeeper who sleeps with you, an occasional lover? How on earth can you suggest that I pretend to be either?'

'I didn't suggest it. Other people will choose the labels and award them as they see fit. But you'll have to have some good reason to still be at Madrigal Court when I move in and start spending a fortune on the place.'

Ophelia was so furious that her teeth chattered together. Her mood was not helped by the reality that he had picked yet another angle that she had not foreseen, for of course people would wonder what was going on when he moved in and she stayed on. Furthermore, while the same people would not dare to ask him impertinent questions, the neighbours were likely to be much more nosy and direct where she was concerned.

'I'm not domesticated enough to be a housekeeper,' she framed grittily.

'It would be an excuse, not a vocation.' Lysander had moved closer without her even being aware of it and she backed a tiny step, her slim hips brushing the arm of the sofa behind her. 'Forget the label. You will know the truth even if nobody else does. You could be staying on to advise me on the gardens.'

'The gardens?' His height and breadth and sheer masculinity had never seemed more pronounced than they did at that moment. Even in heels that gave her a couple of inches she felt overshadowed. Unwarily she collided with eyes that were the rich golden brown and tawny of burnished metal and a pulse at her collarbone flickered out her extreme tension. She couldn't swallow and her mouth ran dry, even while she came to grips with what she interpreted as a genuine suggestion and one with a great deal of appeal.

'Naturally I would pay you for your consulting services.' A wolfish smile slashed his handsome mouth and just for an instant she was totally spellbound, her attention locked to his lean bronzed face.

'You wouldn't have to pay me to get involved in restoring the gardens!' Ophelia told him breathlessly.

Without an atom of hesitation, Lysander curved lean fingers to her slender waist and pulled her to him. 'You would be wasted outdoors, *glikia mou*,' he murmured huskily, then he observed, 'Your heart is pounding like a hammer.'

'Yes.' Never had Ophelia been more conscious of the fact. A little voice was ranting, *No, no, no,* in the back of her head. It sounded remarkably like her grandmother. She knew she shouldn't be that close to him, shouldn't be allowing any form of contact. But she was already driving a sort of devil's bargain with her brain, because she was entrapped by the most indescribably powerful anticipation of what he might do next. Just another few seconds…because she was curious to see what it would be like if he touched her, she reasoned dizzily, just plain ordinary *curious*…

Then he kissed her and the scientific approach of testing him took a hike. That one kiss was ten, a hundred, times more powerful a temptation than any she had withstood before. She trembled as his sensual mouth played with hers. Her temperature rocketed up the scale. She was imprisoned by new sensation. Breath feathering in her lungs, she shifted closer of her own volition. He closed one hand in her hair and held her to his lean, hard body, squashing her breasts, curving her up against his long, hard thighs. Naked excitement whooshed up through her like a firework heading for the heavens. He probed the sensitive interior of her mouth with his tongue and she shuddered with delight. He tasted like the richest and most decadent chocolate, sinful and sexy and forbidden and like any chocoholic she couldn't get enough of the flavour.

His breathing fractured enough to be audible, Lysander

tore himself free. His bronze eyes were molten gold with hunger. He was stunned to register that he was already aroused to the point of pain; his only thought was to alleviate it. 'Come home with me for lunch,' he urged in a roughened undertone.

Shame grabbed Ophelia by the throat and tortured her then and there on the spot. 'You're not talking about lunch, are you?' she mumbled unevenly.

Lysander hauled her back up against him with confident hands, scorching eyes raking her hectically flushed and confused face with masculine satisfaction. '*Theos*... I want you in my bed and under me first.'

The heat inside Ophelia, the wicked pulse of driving, overwhelming desire that had momentarily controlled her, turned colder than yesterday's dinner. He wanted to bed her as no doubt he had bedded countless women. It was lust, nothing more basic, nothing less complimentary. No, he wasn't that particular, but she had always believed that she *was*. Now she had learned differently and the power of what she had felt—the sheer blood-rushing, glorious charge of excitement—had taken her by storm. Her surrender had been terrifyingly immediate.

'No, I don't want this...I'm sorry.' Ophelia forced out that admission in a state of extreme embarrassment.

With the striking animal grace that laced all his movements, Lysander released her. While her sudden rejection astonished him, it also brought a chilling glint of cynical derision to his metallic gaze. He had met many women who calculated that waiting would make him all the more eager for their bodies and all the more generous in the aftermath. Cunning feminine tricks turned him off big time because he had been targeted by innumerable stratagems over the years.

'It's not a problem. The timing is bad,' Lysander murmured. 'I have just one more point to make.'

Ophelia was disconcerted by the ease with which he dismissed that moment of intimacy and moved on. Still all of a quiver inside, she could not bring herself to meet his gaze. Initially relieved by his casual attitude, she could not help feeling insulted a moment later when she found herself thinking that her apparent attraction had proved to be very short-lived. Suddenly, and purely thanks to him, she was at war with herself on every level.

'And that point is?' she prompted, reaching down to relocate her handbag and move in the general direction of the door.

'You need an image makeover.'

Bemused by that assurance, Ophelia turned to study him. 'I beg your pardon?'

'Dressed like that, you won't convince anyone that you're involved with me on any level,' Lysander spelt out.

Ophelia was affronted. She was clean, tidy and presentable. As far as she was concerned, that should be more than sufficient to satisfy. 'There's nothing wrong with my appearance—'

'You require a new wardrobe and better grooming to take on the role. My staff will organise it—'

'But I don't want a new wardrobe—'

'Of course you do.' Arrogant conviction was stamped in every angle of Lysander's lean, darkly handsome face. 'All women love fashion and designer clothes.'

'I don't,' Ophelia told him flatly, wishing she were in a position to tell him what he could do with his talk of image makeovers. But she was intelligent enough to recognise the problem: she was dealing with a guy accustomed to infinitely more decorative women who were always perfectly groomed and exquisitely dressed in the latest fashion. That kind of absorption in her looks wasn't her style and never would be. For the first time she was being forced to appreciate how much control she would be relinquishing over her own life. It was the price, she recognised heavily, of having compromised her principles. He expected her to comply with his every demand.

'Have we a deal?' Lysander asked as though she hadn't spoken.

The silence rushed and surged in Ophelia's ears. Her fingers bit into her palms and she thought about the letter she would receive on her wedding day. Slowly but surely, the almost overwhelming desire to tell Lysander Metaxis where to get off receded. For over eight years Gladys Stewart had stubbornly denied any knowledge of Molly's whereabouts. But what else could be in that letter but information about Molly? A makeover? No, Ophelia was determined not to let pride come between her and her wits.

'Yes, we have a deal,' she said stiffly.

CHAPTER FOUR

COSMETICS had wrought a subtle alteration to Ophelia's face by adding definition and colouring. But to her frowning gaze her eyes and her lips looked uncomfortably prominent. Nor was there any way to hide her hourglass curves in the clinging fabric of the white silk designer confection that she had to wear for the wedding. Leaving her slim shoulders bare, the gown clung like an unwelcome second skin from bosom to knee before flaring out into a frivolous fishtail hem.

'It's so tight I can't sit down,' Ophelia complained thinly.

'Brides aren't supposed to sit down and please don't tell me again that you're not an ordinary bride. Go with the flow,' Pamela urged. 'Remember that when you walk out of the church all your financial worries will be at an end.'

Ophelia tried and failed to smile. 'You should go home now. Thanks for helping out.'

'Shouldn't you be leaving for the church?'

'I'm not in any hurry.'

'Well, if you're sure you don't need me.' Her friend stood up. 'You look totally gorgeous. It's such a shame it's not for real.'

When Pamela had gone, the minutes ticked slowly past while Ophelia paced the floor of the drawing room. The chauffeur, who was waiting for her to come out, knocked twice on the door to tell her worriedly that time was moving on, but she still didn't emerge.

Although only ten days had passed since she had seen Lysander in London, the run-up to the wedding had proved incredibly stressful. Madrigal Court had been awash with strangers who'd conducted surveys, moving furniture and wandering around tapping walls and lifting floorboards. Change had been everywhere she'd looked, but not once had she been asked for her opinion. Two firms had already embarked on emergency repairs and the noisy hum of power tools had put paid to all peace. However, Ophelia had enjoyed the quiet of the walled garden, which she had found unlocked in the evening after she returned from London. Then she had mused rather bitterly that not having slapped his face when he'd kissed her had paid dividends.

Lysander's staff—and he seemed to have an endless supply of them—had toured the house to select virtually all the principal rooms for their employer's occasional use. After agonising over the lack of luxury on offer and the wintry indoor temperatures, they had shipped in several lorry-loads of furniture, lighting, rugs, curtains and bedding in compensation and evidently intended to light an awful lot of fires. Cleaners had arrived to turn the manor house inside out, while a snooty foreign chef and his assistant had imported a free-standing kitchen and had taken up residence in what had once been the servants' hall. Only Haddock was enjoying the fuss and furore of all the new faces and different voices.

In the midst of the domestic upheaval, Ophelia had had to endure the attentions of a squabbling pair of fashion consultants and a team of beauticians, none of whom had appeared to regard her as anything more than an inanimate doll to be painted, polished and repackaged. Lower necklines, shorter skirts, shameless underwear and very high heels were to be the new order of the day. Ophelia had dutifully donned her wedding gown and the frilly underpinnings in a one-day-only act of generosity, but once the ring was on her finger she planned to leave every other item in the wardrobe—though that was not an accurate description for the vast collection of colour-coded new garments currently stored in a separate room.

Lysander had been notable only by his complete absence. They had spoken just once on the phone and only at her instigation, because he had the infuriating habit of passing on reams of instructions to her through his staff. Ophelia had attempted to refuse the vast sum of money offered to her as a reward for signing the pre-nuptial contract in which they'd agreed that, in the event of a divorce, each of them would take out of the marriage only what they brought in. The contract had also specified that she was to receive a whopping great monthly allowance from him. The amount of cash on offer had seemed so ridiculously huge that Ophelia had felt horribly like a gold-digger. After all, Lysander had already settled all the outstanding bills at Madrigal Court. But he had pointed out that the contract had to appear convincing, so he could not reasonably offer her less. Suppressing her misgivings and the niggling suspicion that he didn't really believe in her altruism, she had signed. She was determined to hand all the money back once their agreement was at an end.

Fresh from an unsettling week in his Greek homeland, Lysander flew in for the wedding. It had not been easy to shelve his natural authority in Athens and take on a supportive role while medical personnel took centre stage. He thought it fortunate that he was not the emotional type. Unlike his adoptive father, he was not given to volatile hand-wringing drama. No, thankfully, he had never been that way inclined. There was no weakness in him and if he was currently in an unusually dark frame of mind, he laid that at the door of jet lag and the nuisance value of a stupid secret wedding.

He wondered bleakly how long it would take to turn the ugly duckling house into a convincing swan and even whether there would be enough time. The tenor of that downbeat reflection made him cease that entire train of thought. The helicopter landed in the wooded grounds of the church. There were barely five minutes to spare before the ceremony. His timing was perfect. His legal team would be waiting to act as witnesses and in forty-eight hours he would be on his way again.

But the minutes ticked by in the little country church and the agreed time for the ceremony came and went. The vicar's store of small talk became strained. When fifteen minutes had crawled past, Lysander strode back down the aisle without hesitation. 'I'll fetch her…'

But the bridal limousine was finally drawing up outside. After the chauffeur had sprinted to open the passenger door, Ophelia climbed out slowly, as though she had all the time in the world. A waterfall of heavy golden hair fell round her shoulders and framed her ice-blue eyes and exquisite face in a picture of arresting loveliness. Last time Lysander had seen her she'd had the quality of an uncut diamond; now she was a vision of polished perfection. Perfection on the surface and a grubby little soul of pure avarice underneath, he reminded himself with derision.

'You're late,' Lysander said coldly.

Ophelia shrugged a slight shoulder in defiance and glanced

up the steps at him. Sunlight glinted on his black close-cropped hair, accentuating the proud thrust of his high cheek-bones and the strong angles of his jaw. A dangerous little frisson of response snaked through her pelvis. Pink warmed her cheeks. 'But at least I've turned up.'

Lysander recognised that as a reference to his father having jilted her mother. Not his parent's finest hour, but Aristide had had his reasons and his son did not appreciate the reminder. 'Let's go inside,' Lysander murmured, extending a scrupulously polite hand to her.

His display of good manners made Ophelia squirm and feel petty. His hand engulfed hers in a firm hold. As the service began she was still remembering her mother's unhappy experience and it was like a chill wind blowing over her exposed skin. Yet the words of the marriage service had never seemed more beautiful. She froze when a narrow platinum band was put on her finger and felt a dreadful fraud when the vicar beamed happily at her.

When she climbed back into the limo, a prompting that ran stronger than self-discipline made her look at Lysander. He was gorgeous. His metallic gaze telegraphed an indolent bronzed enquiry that made her heart skip a beat. Hurriedly she glanced away again. When she looked once at those lean, breathtakingly handsome features, she just wanted to look and look again. Indeed the potency of that urge unnerved her. It was as if she had caught a virus that was destroying her common sense and self-control. A sort of sexual infatuation, she labelled in strong embarrassment. Was she more vulnerable because she had never had a lover?

That very acknowledgement irritated Ophelia, who had never believed in dwelling on that reality. She had simply never met anyone she wanted to get that intimate with and dating had always seemed to be more hassle than it was worth, particularly when she recalled she had fallen asleep on a couple of guys over dinner. She had long since reached the conclusion that she was a natural singleton and just not that physical in a world that seemed obsessed with sex. But in the space of two encounters and a single kiss, Lysander Metaxis had shown her just how strong and persuasive carnal temptation could be. That new knowledge was still tugging at her senses and threatening to make a fool of her, she thought ruefully. Hadn't she learned anything from her vulnerable mother's mistakes with men?

As the limo came to a halt outside the manor house Ophelia scrambled out of the car at speed, dodged the waiting photographer and made to speed across the bridge over the moat. She was fully focused on the happy prospect of opening her grandmother's mysterious letter.

'Ophelia…' Lysander murmured *sotto voce*.

Ophelia froze on the bridge. She hated the way he said her name. She hated that quiet expectant note of absolute command, which implied that only the most unforgivably rude or stupid person would dare to defy him. Slowly she turned round and retraced her steps.

'I just don't see the point of these stupid photos,' she vented under her breath.

'Smile,' Lysander urged, closing an arm round her small rigid figure, which had all the yielding qualities of a steel bar. 'You can do better than *that*, Ophelia…'

A few minutes later, he eased her round to face him. She looked up for she could do little else. His eyes were pure glittering gold in the fading light. He leant down and grazed her mouth with the lightest touch of his. With the utmost delicacy he pried apart her full lips to make way for the invasive stroke of his tongue. It was the most erotic experience she had ever had. A second before she had been trying not to shiver from the cooling effects of a brisk April breeze on her bare skin. A second later she was in his arms, ensnared by the onslaught of piercingly sweet pleasure. She trembled, her breath mingling with his, her heart racing so fast she was dizzy. Exhilaration leapt and danced through her veins like stardust.

And then Lysander freed her again. Blinking rapidly, Ophelia recognised the photographer's smiling satisfaction over the shots he had captured before she saw the sardonic amusement that briefly coloured her bridegroom's stunning dark deep-set eyes. Hot, painful pink flooded up below her fine skin. She had forgotten who she was, where she was and why she was acting the part of a bride. But Lysander had forgotten none of those things and his cold opportunism chilled her to the marrow. She shivered. The late afternoon light was fading fast into dusk as she walked back into Madrigal Court.

'I really don't think *that* was necessary,' she said flatly.

'We've cut enough corners,' Lysander fielded drily, annoyed that he had not exercised more restraint. 'The conventional touches will make us look more convincing.'

A waiter greeted them in the porch with a tray bearing a pair of elegant champagne flutes. Ophelia frowned. 'I don't drink.'

Lysander shot her a cool glance and slotted a champagne flute into her hand regardless. 'Make an effort. This is a special occasion.'

Rigid with anger and an awareness of him that inflamed her even more, Ophelia held the flute so tightly she was afraid it would break between her fingers. In a sudden movement she drank the contents down in an unappreciative gulp and set the glass down again. No doubt it wouldn't do her any harm this once. She looked around: the Great Hall was full of lawyers enjoying the generous array of drinks and food on offer. Lysander was soon engulfed by his legal team, so Ophelia headed straight for her solicitor.

Haddock announced his presence in the corner by breaking into an off-key rendering of 'Here Comes the Bride'. Heads turned, supercilious brows lifting. Ophelia almost groaned out loud, for she had brought the parrot upstairs only because he was lonely in the kitchen. Unfortunately that well-known melody sent a chill down Ophelia's spine because she had grown up with a mother who always burst into tears when she heard it. She continued her journey over to her solicitor.

'I have the letter here,' Donald Morton told her cheerfully.

'Thanks.' Ophelia clutched the surprisingly fat envelope and hesitated before ripping it open. When she unfolded the document within, a small piece of notepaper that had been attached to it fluttered free and fell to the floor. She bent to scoop it up and frowned when she saw the single handwritten sentence it carried.

Molly had been put up for adoption.

There was nothing else, no opening preamble, no signature, nothing other than that brief bald admission in her grandmother's spidery scrawl.

Ophelia was shaken by a possibility that she had not previously considered. Her sibling had been adopted? Had the story about Molly's father taking her only been a convenient piece of fiction? Ophelia stilled while she pondered: unless Molly chose to look into her own past and seek out birth relatives, Ophelia's sister might well be lost to her for ever. Her eyes stung with sudden tears of regret and frustration. She looked numbly down at the other document in her hand and read the first few lines of it over and over again before she could accept what she was reading. Disbelief attacked her and she re-approached her solicitor, who was being served with food at the buffet.

'There's what looks like another will in the envelope,' she told him shakily.

The older man was astonished and he immediately set down his plate. 'May I have a look?'

Still bound up in her disappointment, Ophelia passed over the document. She knew she should have known better than to get her hopes up about the letter. While she had finally learned the truth behind her sister's disappearance, she felt as if Molly was more out of her reach than ever.

'May I speak to you in the drawing room, Miss Carter… sorry, er, Mrs Metaxis?' Donald Morton had assumed his more formal manner again. Ophelia and her solicitor were fast becoming the centre of attention and silence was slowly spreading across the Great Hall.

'Metaxis bounder—good-for-nothing swine!' Haddock squawked with gleeful abandon. 'There'll never be a Metaxis at Madrigal Court!'

Impervious to the shock value of Haddock's announcement, Ophelia watched dully as Donald Morton approached one of the other lawyers. A look of consternation crossed the man's face and he quickly went into a huddle with his colleague.

The drawing room was now barely recognisable to Ophelia. Its former shabbiness and clutter had been banished in favour of wonderful paintings and handsome furniture. Beautiful curtains hung at the windows. She pressed clammy hands to her tense face. The implications of the existence of another will were finally sinking in. What new torment had Gladys Stewart planned with the provision of a second will that would invalidate the first, if it post-dated it?

'Ophelia…' Lean, strong face hard, Lysander strode into the room and towards her. 'What is happening? What is this about? A *second* will?'

'I don't know…I really don't know,' she said tautly, dragging her attention away from him, hastily burying the memory of that wide sensual mouth playing with hers. Playing was the operative word, she told herself unhappily. She had let her guard down. She hastily buried the reflection that she was now married to Lysander. The very thought embarrassed her, trespassing as it did over the barriers she was determined to erect in her mind. It wasn't a marriage; it was an 'arrangement'.

Lysander startled Ophelia by closing a lean hand over hers when she tried to turn away. Flustered and flushed, she collided with his brilliant questioning gaze and snaked her fingers free, turning her head away in angry discomfiture. She suppressed the sense of connection she felt to him, stamping it out like a spark that threatened to cause a conflagration. There might be a ring on her finger but, in essence, it was meaningless.

Donald Morton arrived to confirm, 'Mrs Stewart appears to have had another will drawn up by a London firm. It's signed and witnessed and it is of a more recent date.'

'Which means it takes precedence over the first,' Lysander said flatly.

'You're not mentioned as a beneficiary in this will, Mr Metaxis,' the older man told him heavily.

Ophelia frowned. 'Then what does it say?'

A few minutes later, Ophelia sank down on a nearby chair because her knees felt too weak to support her. She was too stunned to know quite what she was feeling—her grandmother had left her Madrigal Court in its entirety.

Cold wrath held Lysander still and silent, his attention shooting straight to his bride. Ophelia didn't look at him. There she sat, delicate as a tiny porcelain doll with baby-blue eyes, in an attitude of shock. Lysander wasn't impressed. Of course she must have known about the second will! The very fact that he was forced to operate within time constraints had given Ophelia an advantage, Lysander reflected rawly. He had gone against legal advice in pushing the marriage through so quickly. If background checks on the Stewart family had been made, they might have revealed facts that would have given him pause for thought or picked up on the late Mrs Stewart's dealings with another legal firm. But, be that as it may, Lysander was quick to regroup under threat; he always had a contingency plan to fall back on.

The Metaxis legal team joined them. The situation was discussed in Greek. When the lawyers began to wrangle in two languages, Ophelia rose and went back out to the Great Hall. Honest and straightforward as she was, she was appalled by the cruel cunning of her grandmother's trickery.

'Hello, Ophelia,' Haddock said chirpily.

Ophelia took the parrot back down to the kitchen. She recalled Gladys Stewart's triumphant forecast that Madrigal Court would make her granddaughter's every hope and dream come true. But Ophelia had dreamt only of being able to find her sister and the freedom to get on with her life. And that latter dream she had never shared with anyone, as it had made her feel guilty. That she had unwittingly become the instrument of her grandmother's revenge appalled her. The older woman had not cared who might suffer when it came to striking a lethal blow against the Metaxis family. She had set up her granddaughter alongside the son of her greatest enemy. The end result was unarguable: Lysander Metaxis had married Ophelia for nothing!

Ophelia pondered the explosive truth that *she* was now the new and outright owner of Madrigal Court! But before a sense of joy could take hold of her, the most awful guilt assailed her instead. Because of the terms of the previous will, Lysander had been expecting her to sell her share of the house to him and, of course, she could not have afforded to do otherwise. The entire picture had changed, however; now that the whole house was hers, surely she had more options. A heady sense of challenge was already bubbling inside her. Could Madrigal Court be turned into a paying proposition so that she could keep her inheritance? What the heck was she going to do? What was fair? And would she still be fair to Lysander, even if being so meant going against her own inclinations?

The guests had departed and the house seemed eerily silent when Ophelia finally walked back up the basement stairs. Darkness had fallen and elegant new lamps glowed in corners. She almost switched them off to save electric and then winced, recognising how engrained her need to save money had become. Lysander was poised by the giant stone fireplace in the Great Hall. She came to an abrupt halt, apprehension gripping her, for she still had no idea what her ultimate decision would be.

'Where did you sneak off to?' Lysander demanded icily.

Ophelia bristled like a cat stroked the wrong way. 'I didn't *sneak* anywhere! I had to have a chance to think things over.'

Bronze eyes dark and hard as granite, Lysander focused on her with punitive force. She had yet to learn that he fought fire with greater fire. She couldn't win against him. Nobody ever did and many had tried. His attention lingered on the luscious curve of her lips and the ripe swell of her pale breasts above the silk bodice of her wedding gown. He remembered the feel and the taste of her. Sexual heat pooled in his groin and sizzling anticipation burned the edge off his anger.

Ophelia felt horribly uncomfortable and guilty even though she knew that she had done nothing wrong. 'You have every right to be livid. I'm very sorry about this situation.'

His cold contemptuous gaze cloaked, Lysander studied the brandy swirling in the fine glass between his fingers. Of course she wasn't sorry. He had no doubt that she planned to hold the house like a gun to his head to achieve the highest possible sale price. He wondered how generous and sweet she would feel when she realised how powerless she really was. She had overlooked a powerful counterbalance: she was his wife. While she might not be behaving like a wife as yet, she would soon learn her boundaries.

The tense silence pounded in Ophelia's eardrums and played havoc with her nerves. When she could stand it no longer she broke into speech. 'After my mother was jilted, my grandmother became obsessed with the idea of getting her own back on your family. Perhaps I didn't take her feelings seriously enough,' she conceded heavily. 'But then I didn't see how she could do any real damage and I had no idea that she was capable of going to these lengths—'

'It's too late for lies.' His rich dark accented drawl roughened the tenor of that warning. 'You must've known there were two wills. You played a starring role in your grandmother's revenge because she made it financially worth your while to do so.'

Ophelia was shattered that he could suspect her of having been a party to her grandmother's deception from the outset. 'That's not true. For a start, she didn't confide in me and I—'

'You're wasting your time trying to act innocent—'

'For goodness' sake, it's not an act! Why should I have known that there was another will? How could I have guessed that?' Dry-mouthed, Ophelia lifted what she thought was a bottle of water from the bar set up in one corner and filled a glass to drink. But when the liquid hit her throat, her eyes watered and she had to swallow fast and painfully to ward off an embarrassing fit of coughing and spluttering, because what she had mistaken for water was actually alcohol.

His lean, tanned face harsh, Lysander watched his bride knock back a large shot of neat vodka. He recalled her prim insistence that she did not drink and he wondered how he had believed for one second that he could trust her.

'You're misjudging me,' Ophelia told him steadfastly.

'I don't think so.'

Lysander had a hauteur that even royalty would have been challenged to equal and he did derision to the manner born as well. Stung raw by his cold look of incredulity, Ophelia wanted to shout, while at the same time wanting to squirm. With taut hands she opened a genuine bottle of water to rinse the acrid taste of alcohol from her mouth. 'Believe me, I knew nothing about any of this,' she argued. 'I was never that close to my grandmother.'

'You were close enough for her to leave you everything she possessed. All you had to do to win that prize was play along with her warped plans and go through with marrying me.'

Ophelia spun angrily back to him. 'You're the one who asked *me* to marry *you*! How can you accuse me of having plotted this?'

'Easily. Even your parrot is obsessed with revenge,' Lysander derided.

Her crystalline eyes flared. 'Just you leave Haddock out of this!'

His deep, dark eyes were cold as the depths of a river. 'Let's cut to the bottom line—how much will it cost me to buy the house from you?'

Colouring beneath the contempt etched in his lean strong face, Ophelia flung her golden head high. 'I'm not even sure I'm willing to sell it any more!'

His worst expectations and darkest suspicions confirmed by that statement, Lysander murmured something sibilant in Greek. The tense silence hung like a sheet of glass about to crash.

'Everything's changed!' Ophelia was struggling not to be intimidated by his mood and the daunting force of will he emanated. 'And it's not my fault.'

'Isn't it?' Lysander breathed. 'Even your supposed reluctance to marry me was faked to allay any suspicions I might have had of your motives.'

'I didn't fake anything! My grandmother fooled me as well and landed me into this mess with you!' Ophelia flung back with spirit.

'But it's a very lucrative mess from your point of view. You qualified for your inheritance and you'll profit even more from the pre-nuptial contract you signed with me.'

Eyes bright with anger, Ophelia snatched in a sustaining breath. 'I wasn't planning on accepting that cash…*actually*—'

Lysander loosed a derisive laugh. 'I liked you better when you were honest about your love of money.'

'Oh, did you indeed? So you're still fully convinced that I'm a thoroughly grasping little gold-digger, are you?' Her nails biting into her palms, Ophelia shot him a look of seething resentment.

Black-lashed metallic eyes rested on her in cutting consideration. 'You said it, *glikia mou.*'

Temper shot through Ophelia's slender frame like an adrenalin charge, since there was no way that she could prove that she hadn't known about the two wills. He infuriated her and the urge to outdo him and have the last word ruled supreme. She was fed up with being pushed around and insulted. She had apologised, she had tried to explain and he wasn't interested. Well, she was done with being humble with this guy, who had now accused her of being a fraud, a liar and a cheat! If he wanted to believe that she was an evil, greedy schemer, he was welcome to.

'Well, that's all right then,' Ophelia fired back full throttle. 'I'll rip you off for every penny I can get because that's exactly what you deserve!'

'You can *try.*' A dark light had kindled in Lysander's bronze gaze. Her defiance, allied with that overconfident admission, hurled the kind of challenge that no woman had ever dared to give him. He was used to soft words and submission, flattery and feminine coaxing.

'You're a bad loser.' Ophelia was in no mood to take back her angry words. Just then the guise of a gutsy gold-digger seemed infinitely preferable to continuing to whine that she had known nothing about anything. Anyway, what use was the truth with a guy who refused to listen?

'Naturally. But be warned, I'm superb at turning a losing hand into a winning one,' Lysander countered smooth as glass.

'I'm going upstairs to get out of this stupid dress!' Ophelia flung back at him, out of all patience.

An urgent knock sounded on the door into the outer hall. As it was already lying open, Ophelia wondered who had been outside listening to the bridal couple fight like cat and dog and she reddened. A heavily built older man with a troubled expression appeared on the threshold. He gave her a respectful nod of acknowledgement and then turned to address Lysander in a voluble flood of Greek. Ophelia walked away—while Lysander discovered that the bad news wasn't over yet.

CHAPTER FIVE

'OPHELIA!' Lysander growled just as Ophelia reached the top of the carved staircase. 'Come down.'

For a split second, Ophelia hesitated. That note of command bit at her resolve. But she was now in full resistance mode to Metaxis authority and so she sped on. She reminded herself that she wasn't really and truly married to Lysander, except on paper, and every passing minute was giving her another good reason to celebrate that truth.

'Game over,' Lysander breathed rawly, striding past her to block her passage down the corridor.

'Games are fun…being married to you is anything but!' Ophelia hurled back. 'Now get out of my way!'

'I have questions I want answered,' Lysander imparted.

'What you want isn't always what you get—let me past.'

Lysander stayed where he was, his lean muscular frame as large, still and formidable as a cliff face. The atmosphere hummed.

Enraged at his persistence, Ophelia tried to sidestep him, but when he remained in her path she gave him a tiny meaningful push. In answer to that very restrained hint that he remove himself at speed, Lysander closed his hands round her waist and lifted her right off her feet.

'Put me down!' Ophelia shouted at the top of her voice, feeling remarkably foolish with her legs dangling.

'Not until you cool off.' Arms outstretched as he held her back from him, Lysander studied her with icy self-containment.

'You're behaving like a bully!' Ophelia snapped furiously across the narrow divide that separated them.

'You assaulted me,' Lysander drawled, lush ebony lashes low above eyes that were blaze-bronze.

Ophelia was thoroughly disconcerted by that reminder. She collided with his smouldering gaze and it was as if all the air that there was to breathe had suddenly burned up in the atmosphere. Warmth curled through her in an enervating surge that scared her. 'I'm calm,' she framed, taken aback by a physical response that even rage couldn't suppress.

Lysander lowered her to the floor again with exaggerated care. Anger was storming around like a caged animal inside him. He had planned to confine the marriage to one tiny compartment of his life and now that convenient arrangement was no longer possible. Even worse, he would have to maintain the pretence for the benefit of his family. 'The grounds are crawling with paparazzi,' he imparted.

'Papa-what? Oh, those photographers that chase celebrities,' Ophelia mumbled, her brows having pleated in momentary mystification. 'What are they doing here? Oh, right, they followed you down from London—'

His scorching eyes were welded to her. 'No. Try again.'

'Try what?'

'Acting dumb. So far you're not being very convincing.'

'What are you trying to insinuate?' Ophelia took the opportunity to snake past him with the agility of an eel. 'Well, I'm not listening to one more nonsensical word!'

As Ophelia thrust open the door of her bedroom Lysander closed a hand like a steel manacle round her narrow wrist.

'Tomorrow the newspapers will be full of the story of our marriage,' he breathed in a wrathful undertone.

Wide-eyed, Ophelia turned back to look at him, his imprisoning hold forgotten. 'Did they find out about the two wills as well?'

'No. Only that we got married today, which is more than sufficient.'

'But *how* did it get out? I mean, we've taken such care—'

Lysander studied her with sizzling force. 'Stamitos, my head of security, already has a suspect and it isn't anyone in my employ. The story was leaked by someone who knew the score. The woman who lives in the gatehouse—your friend...'

'Pamela Arnold? What's she got to do with this?'

'She has a brother who works on a tabloid newspaper.'

'Yes, but she hardly ever sees him.' But dismay at that reminder had frozen Ophelia to the spot and she had paled. Although she had sworn her friend to secrecy, she was painfully aware that Pamela had found the entire wedding scenario, not to mention Lysander's wealth, hugely exciting. Nobody loved to talk more than Pamela. Could her friend have accidentally let information slip in the wrong quarter?

'By tomorrow morning the whole world will know that I have taken a wife.'

'I really don't think the whole world is likely to be that interested.' An uneasy conscience, however, ensured that Ophelia's comeback was less feisty than usual. Then her thoughts were sidetracked by the startling discovery that her bedroom looked unfamiliar—the bed had been stripped and her possessions were no longer in view. 'Where have my things gone?'

'What are you talking about?'

'Half my stuff has vanished from my room!'

'Wives don't sleep on the other side of the house.'

Her hackles came up, since nobody had consulted her on what she assumed to be a move to another bedroom. 'I'm not a wife.'

'You are now and it's obvious that the status of being my wife is what you wanted all along.' His lean, tanned face granite hard, Lysander turned her back to him. 'Clearly you planned the maximum possible exposure for our marriage in the media.'

Ophelia discovered that she was fighting a very irrational urge to giggle. Just at that instant she didn't feel she could have planned her way out of an open space. The alcohol she had imbibed had gone straight to her head, for she had had nothing to eat since breakfast. 'You're so distrustful—of course I didn't plan it! Why would I have wanted people to know about this crazy arrangement?'

'So that you could become my wife in reality.'

'In reality? Meaning?' Ophelia queried as he strode down the passage, trailing her willy-nilly in his wake.

Lysander swung into the Long Gallery. 'Plan B is about to go into operation.'

'Plan B? Where on earth are you taking me?'

Lysander thrust wide the door of Madrigal Court's principal bedroom. The huge room had not been used by Ophelia's family, who had found the Victorian wing at the back of the house easier to heat. Now a fire leapt and glowed in the giant grate below the stone chimneypiece, sending shadows snaking and flickering over the oak-panelled walls. A fabulous four-poster bed, wholly in keeping with the feudal splendour of the new décor, sat centre stage.

Ophelia had never been the slightest bit domesticated. She was untouched by any desire to rearrange the furniture or shop for new curtains, but she had occasionally been conscious of a wistful yearning for her surroundings to be warmer, more comfortable and inviting. Now she stared in astonishment at the imposing bed, draped in flamboyant golden fabric.

'Your employees have contrived the most amazing transformation. I've been so busy in the garden I haven't had the chance to keep up with all the improvements.' Her smooth brow indented. 'Why did you bring me in here?'

'This is our room.'

'*Our*…room?'

Lysander shot Ophelia a long, lingering appraisal that made her skin prickle. 'The marital bedroom.'

'We don't have a marital bedroom because, well…what would we do with one?' An uneasy laugh was wrenched from Ophelia, who was recalling his crack about the sort of boots he liked a woman to wear. She really didn't like his sense of humour.

'All the usual things, *glikia mou*,' Lysander murmured lazily. 'Not much else to do at this season in the country and at least it would keep us warm.'

'Let me get this straight…you are expecting me to share a room with you?' Ophelia gasped.

Grim amusement gripped Lysander. She was amazingly good at acting the naïve country girl while simultaneously contriving to look quite extraordinarily beautiful. 'Even if our marriage had remained our secret we would still have had to share a room when I was here. How else could we ever have pretended that it was a normal marriage?'

Ophelia was bemused. 'But I had no idea you were expecting me to share a room with you!'

'We have an agreement.'

'Yes, but everything has changed now—'

'Only the will. You are still my wife and, since that is no longer a secret, we are much more married than I ever expected to be,' Lysander delineated with cold emphasis.

Discomfited pink winged across her cheeks. 'Yes, I appreciate that.'

Lifting a lean, elegant hand, Lysander skimmed the troubled pout of her upper lip with a careless fingertip. 'Do you?'

Her colour fluctuated and her tummy turned a somersault. The deeper note in his rich dark drawl reverberated down her taut spine. It took conscious effort not to lean closer and invite further contact. 'Other people knowing about us will make a difference.'

'More than a difference. Marriage has never been on my to-do list. I enjoy my freedom,' Lysander continued, 'but for the foreseeable future I have no choice other than to behave like a newly married man.'

Now Ophelia sensed the inner tempest of the emotions that he had previously kept hidden; neither Gladys's second will nor the paparazzi had provoked him into a loss of temper. Firelight gilded his eyes to pure gold and threw his strong bone structure into prominence. He was a natural born predator, she reflected helplessly, and as dazzling and dangerous as a glossy jungle cat in his prime. Even when every inner alarm bell was urging her to back off she couldn't bring herself to do it.

'I'm surprised you have so much respect for the conventions.'

'Only in that one field, *glikia mou*.' Lysander slid long brown fingers into her hair and eased her up against him with a calm belied by the heat of his gaze. He was already fiercely aroused: he wanted her. The angrier she made him, the more he wanted her and the more determined he became to stamp her as his. He didn't understand the connection but he didn't waste any time thinking about it either. Any thought and any desire that had a sexual angle was self-explanatory and absolutely natural in Lysander's opinion.

Her heart was pounding, her breath fluttering in her throat. As her slim body connected with his hard muscular frame a dozen pulse points of desire were ignited. She was so tense her lower limbs felt numb and she had to dig her fingers into his shoulder to stay upright. A battle was being fought inside her. She knew she should retreat but the bold challenge of his bronze eyes and the sweet taunting heaviness low in her pelvis kept her where she was.

He brought his sensual mouth slowly down to hers. Impatience grabbed her and she strained up to him on tiptoe without even thinking about it. A husky laugh sounded low in his throat. In a total change of approach, he plundered her mouth with a passion that left her dizzy. The erotic thrust of his tongue made her tremble and cling, response leaping through her with firecracker energy.

Between driving kisses, Lysander shed his tie and shrugged out of his jacket. He closed his hands over hers and tugged her towards the bed.

Doubtful, Ophelia said anxiously, 'This can't be right—'

'*Theos*—what could be more right?' Lysander reasoned. 'This is our wedding night.'

That truth silenced her for an instant. 'But I don't feel married.'

'You soon will.' His arrogant dark head bent and he pried her lips apart for another heady taste that made her senses swim.

'But you think I'm a liar and a ch-cheat,' she stammered.

Lysander angled a wolfish smile down at her. 'Nothing's perfect in this world.'

His smile had a charisma that welded her gaze to his lean, darkly handsome features. 'Be serious. I don't even like you!'

Lysander laughed out loud. 'But you want me the same way I want you. From the first look the first day you saw me, *yineka mou.*'

The awesome truth of that instant contradiction cut through Ophelia's protests like a knife. The hunger had started in the same second she had first laid eyes on him. An unsettling, embarrassing, maddening hunger that bore no resemblance to anything she had ever felt before. It was a visceral reaction that had nothing to do with conscious consideration. In any case, she registered in belated acknowledgement, he was never absent from her thoughts for longer than a few minutes. Just when had she become so obsessed with him?

Lysander bent down and lifted her and settled her down on the bed. 'You think too much,' he told her.

'Possibly…' Ophelia watched him remove her dainty bridal shoes. She couldn't quite believe that she was allowing him to do that. Exhilaration bubbled through her while her mind continued to race. She was wondering if she could allow herself to succumb, if it would be so very wrong to sleep with him. Was it wicked to be curious? In terms of pure physical attraction, he was definitely *the one*. She wasn't a romantic like her late mother. She wasn't going to go falling in love with him or anything stupid like that, she told herself. She knew his limitations and accepted them. He was only suitable as a one-night stand. A week of fidelity would be a long-term commitment for him.

'Do you mind me asking…?' Ophelia hesitated.

'Asking what?'

'If you're currently involved with someone else?' Ophelia almost winced as she spoke.

Engaged in unbuttoning his shirt and casting it aside, Lysander suppressed a groan of disbelief. '*Theos*…you make everything so complicated! No, there is no one else at present.'

Ophelia noticed how careful he was to qualify that declaration with the words 'at present'. A muscular brown strip of male chest appeared between the parted edges of his mono-grammed shirt. Her mouth went dry. He dropped the shirt on the floor and edged her round to unhook her dress. She almost stopped breathing. It was one thing to watch him as though he were a pin-up guy on a poster, but quite another thing to imagine getting naked with him. And the prospect of acquiring an audience for the fancy lingerie she wore was even more disquieting.

'You're very tense…' Lysander unfastened the delicate bra that banded her pale narrow back and stood her up again.

She looked down at her bare breasts and hurriedly away again, only just resisting a prompting to cover her naked flesh with her hands. She considered telling him that he would be her first lover and swiftly discarded the idea. He might not believe her and if he did he might think her lack of experience was funny. Even worse, he might think that no man had ever been that interested in her. Every fear that could occur to her at such a moment up to and including a fear of pregnancy was piling up inside her mind when her dress fell round her ankles and he lifted her out of the puddle of white silk.

'Oh…' she gasped, settled back down on the bed, her slender body alternately taut and quivering with nervous energy.

'Oh…' Lysander mimicked wickedly, dipping his imperious dark head to slide his tongue in a provocative invasion between her swollen lips.

Her hips jerked in immediate reflex reaction, damp heat surging between her slender thighs. He explored the ripe swell of her rounded breasts and toyed with the tender peaks. A melting, tingling wave of response took hold of her.

'Luscious,' he growled with masculine satisfaction.

As Lysander studied her pale curves an enervating mixture of pleasure and self-consciousness battled inside Ophelia. Her face burned. He closed his lips round a pointed pink nipple and she almost cried out in startled response. Her body wouldn't stay still for her. Her fingers buried themselves into the silky thickness of his close-cropped black hair and her back arched. He lifted his head again and drove her lips apart with devouring hunger. She loved the way he kissed. It was addictive. Her hands dropped to the corded strength of his strong shoulders. Her mind was a blur of half-formed thoughts. She couldn't credit the strength of what she was feeling or the power of her need to touch him.

Lysander lifted his tousled head to look down at her. Below the black fringe of his lashes, his smouldering dark gaze was intent. He ran long brown fingers through the glossy coils of golden hair spilling across the pillow. He was enjoying his new right to touch. Her bewitching ice-blue eyes shone against skin with the luminous quality of a pearl. 'You looked incredible in that dress today,' he told her.

Disconcerted by that comment, Ophelia blinked. Lysander frowned because he had not intended to compliment her. Feeling off balance, he crushed the strawberry ripeness of her voluptuous mouth under his. Her senses swam and proper thought got lost behind a mental fog. A torrent of energising impressions struck her—the rippling power of his muscles beneath her hands, the long, lean, hair-roughened strength of his thighs and the intrinsically wonderful and familiar scent of him. The weight of him against her felt glorious. The feel of his bold erection shocked and pleased her. And the whole time she was learning about him, her blood was drumming in her eardrums and her heartbeat accelerating as the pleasure became more and more intense.

She didn't even notice her remaining garments being removed. All honeyed heat and response, she reacted by instinct to the pulsing ache at the junction of her thighs. He skimmed through the pale curls that crowned her mound and teased the tiny sensitive bud beneath. Her ability to think vanished. In the grip of his sensual expertise she whimpered and angled up her hips. Desire was becoming a burning, irresistible need. He traced the slick wet heat at the heart of her and exquisite sensation engulfed her in wave after wave. Caught up in out-of-control excitement, she craved a completion she had never known before.

'You're very small,' Lysander murmured.

Ophelia looked up at him in bewilderment for an instant before realising what he meant. 'I'm a virgin…' And the instant the admission left her she tensed and closed her eyes because ironically, no matter how intimate being in bed with him was, that information felt as if it was much too private to share.

Not for one moment did Lysander credit her claim, but he

didn't argue because at that moment he didn't care what she was. Her fervent response to him had stoked his hunger for her to a ravenous height. A sheen of sweat on his bronzed skin and with hands that were rather less steady and controlled than usual, he parted her legs and came over her.

When he began entering her, Ophelia tensed and gasped, for he felt impossibly large. Desire and panic took her in equal parts. 'If it hurts too much you'll have to stop,' she warned him and a split second later, 'You're *hurting*!'

His breathing fracturing with the effort that restraint demanded, his big, powerful body trembling over hers, Lysander stilled and stared down at her in shock and growing awe. 'You were serious. You're really tiny—'

'Stop!' Ophelia recoiled from the sharp stab of pain.

'A virgin…' Studying her with laser-beam intensity and potent appreciation, Lysander closed one large hand over hers. 'I'll be gentle…I promise, *yineka mou*.'

Ophelia discovered that being looked at with awe was rather pleasant. And just for once he was doing as he was told while at the same time accepting that she had told him the truth. Her body was adjusting a little to the intrusion of his and the throbbing ache of hunger was stirring again.

'I'm mad for you,' Lysander growled, his accent thick and deep as his long brown fingers toyed abstractedly with the wedding ring she wore. 'Don't make me stop.'

For the first time Ophelia was conscious of her feminine power and it was as intoxicating as the desire tingling back at every pulse point. 'All right,' she framed in a driven whisper.

Lysander shifted in a subtle move and she squeezed her eyes tight shut as he slowly, carefully sank deeper. It hurt and she cried out. He paused and cupped her face with his hands, then kissed her with a honeyed eroticism that somehow made her bite back the next moan. He murmured in Greek, bronze eyes like flames as she looked up at him. A ripple of pleasure rewarded her for her stoicism. When she had taken all of him, the burn of his possession faded and excitement quivered through her taut figure.

'You feel like velvet,' he told her with hoarse appreciation.

She had neither the breath nor the concentration to find words to describe what she was feeling. Sensual delight made her strain up to him, desire licking through her in a hot, feverish surge. He sank into her again and again with long, measured strokes. Sensation piled on wonderful sensation, stoking her excitement to incredible heights. Trembling with need, she cried out, her entire being caught up in the frantic climb to satisfaction. At a spellbinding peak, melting ripples of ecstasy consumed her in an explosive climax. Lost in the sweet drowning pleasure that followed, she lay in his arms in a daze.

A virgin, Lysander savoured with admiration, and pressed a kiss on her smooth brow. He was conscious of a rare sense of well-being and an even greater sense of satisfaction with her. It was the most extraordinary sensual experience he had ever had. He knew virginity shouldn't count in the balance of her sins but somehow it *did*. Whatever other faults she might have she didn't sleep around. All of a sudden marriage felt less like a trap and more like an indulgence. It was quite some time since his sex life had delivered the satisfaction he had once taken for granted. Women had become a faceless interchangeable blur, all too similar in type and behaviour, he acknowledged grudgingly. His bride was, at least, an original. He laughed huskily, thinking how easy it was to turn a negative into a positive. All it took was a creative and innovative mind.

That soft masculine laugh thrust Ophelia rudely back to reality at the same time as Lysander lifted her over him with easy strength and draped her across his chest like a rag doll. Shifting to a cooler spot in the bed, he kicked off the sheet. Oh, my word, what have I done? Ophelia asked herself in guilty horror. A one-night stand, she reminded herself, but the memory of that insane piece of self-justification only made her want to cringe with embarrassed self-loathing. She had surrendered to the enemy and he would never take her seriously again. She could have screamed with vexation.

'I need a shower…and *then*…' Lysander murmured thickly, running an intimate hand down over the curve of her bottom.

Ophelia rolled off him as though she had been assaulted and flipped round. 'And then…*nothing*!' she stressed in a tight undertone. 'This was a one-off. A colossal mistake. Please don't ask me to explain myself.'

Lysander regarded her with scientific interest and considerable amusement. He would not have dreamt of asking a woman to explain herself, especially one with as much to say for herself as Ophelia. He had discovered that her Achilles' heel was her essential lack of sexual experience and being Lysander he was unlikely to overlook that vulnerability. Ebony lashes low over glittering metallic eyes, he murmured wickedly, 'You were *so* hot—'

'Shut up—don't you dare gloat! I don't want to talk about this *ever*!' Scarlet to the roots of her tumbling golden hair, Ophelia scrambled off the bed and went in frantic search of something to wear.

'Where are you going?'

'Back to my own room.'

'That's not allowed.'

Clutching his jacket in front of her to shield her naked body, Ophelia flung him an irate glance. 'None of that stuff counts now. I don't have to go along with this marriage, if I don't want to. I'm sorry, but you must see that everything we agreed to is redundant now.'

In a lithe lazy movement, Lysander leant up on one elbow. Sprawled naked in the tangled sheet, he was a magnificent vision of bronzed masculinity. He regarded her with level dark-as-midnight eyes and a curious little chill ran down her spine. 'We have a deal,' he reminded her very softly.

Ophelia wrapped both arms round his jacket to hold it in place and couldn't help wishing she'd picked up something more appropriate. 'Yes, but that—'

'No argument, no compromise possible,' Lysander cut in with ruthless bite. 'Before the wedding you agreed that if our marriage went public you would act the part of my wife. It's too late to change your mind.'

The cold implacability of his gaze took Ophelia aback but she refused to back down. 'I'm sorry things aren't turning out the way you expected but that can't be helped. I'm afraid you can't make me go along with the pretence that our marriage is real if I don't want to.'

'We have a deal. If you try to break it, I'll destroy you. You promised to live up to that ring on your finger and you *will*,' Lysander asserted with chilling cool, while he wondered what the hell she was playing at. 'There is no alternative, *glikia mou*.'

Ophelia was clutching his jacket so hard her hands were hurting. 'I don't react well to threats.'

'If you cross me, I will go to court over the two wills and keep you tied up there for so long that when you finally sell Madrigal Court you'll owe all the money you make on legal bills. Complex lawsuits can drag on for years and the expenses of a court battle will bankrupt you. Is that what you want?'

Every scrap of colour had drained from Ophelia's face by the time he had completed that speech. He had totally shocked her. It had not occurred to her that if she refused to honour their previous agreement he might be prepared to drag her into a courtroom to contest the will. Moreover, the scenario he painted horrified her. The inheritance she hoped to share with her sister would be eaten up within months. Nobody would profit from that denouement.

Lysander was on full alert, reading every nuance and change of expression on her delicate features. He had assumed she had played an active role in ensuring that the paparazzi exposed their marriage because only publicity could gain her full access to his rarefied world of exclusive privilege and luxury. Now he was no longer so sure.

Dark eyes sardonic, he sprang off the bed and straightened to his full intimidating height. 'You have to respect ground rules with me,' he spelt out. 'Keep your word and you will have nothing to fear. You're my wife and I will treat my wife like a princess. But if you choose to step out of that charmed circle, beware because it's a cruel world out there.'

'You can't do this to me!' Ophelia snapped with a vehement shake of her head.

'I'm going for a shower. When I return, I still expect you to be in this room as befits a bride on her wedding night,' Lysander informed her lazily. 'And tomorrow we're leaving on our honeymoon.'

Ophelia glowered at him in frank disbelief. 'A honeymoon…you've got to be joking! This is my home. I'm not going anywhere. And what about my plants? Who's going to take care of them? The busiest season of the year is coming up for me. You can't expect me to leave.'

'You're creasing my jacket,' Lysander told her gently.

CHAPTER SIX

WRAPPED in Lysander's discarded shirt, Ophelia discovered her new wardrobe stored in the room next door, which was furnished as a dressing room.

Lysander had switched from passion and seeming tenderness to threat at a speed that had shaken Ophelia to her conservative core. She hated him, she truly hated him. She didn't know what had made her behave so stupidly with him when all her life to date she had been strong and sensible. So why had she slept with a guy who cared nothing for her? Didn't she know any better than that? What had happened to her self-respect? Hadn't she known all along what a rotten reputation he had?

Angry tears stung her shamed eyes while she freshened up in a freezing cold shallow bath in a bathroom along the corridor. How dared he threaten her with the full weight of the law? How dared he use his wealth and power as a weapon against her? As she slid into faded cotton pyjamas she pondered her predicament and struggled to ignore the dulled ache of discomfort that reminded her of the intimacy she was determined to forget.

The idea that she could turn Madrigal Court into a paying proposition on her current income was a total fantasy, she admitted with pained honesty. The house was in need of extensive restoration work, which she could not afford. Besides, she was already in debt to the tune of many thousands of pounds to Lysander, who had paid all her outstanding bills, not to mention the current emergency repairs being done. Unhappily, selling up was her only option. If she conceded that point surely he would drop the demand that she continue acting as his wife? Was he using that to put pressure on her into agreeing to sell?

Lysander was on the phone when Ophelia reappeared. Clad in a pair of boxers and a T-shirt, he was reclining on the bed while one manservant built up the fire and another hovered with a trolley of food. Self-conscious in the face of that invasion, Ophelia fled back into the dressing room to find a wrap. When she emerged again, he was alone.

Tossing aside the phone, Lysander extended a lean brown hand to her. 'Join me,' he urged.

Ophelia froze like a dieter offered a pile of chocolate bars. 'No, I'm not getting into that bed again.'

Stunning heavily lashed metallic eyes rested on her. 'It's your bed. A wedding present from me to you, *yineka mou*.'

'Are you trying to say that you *always* planned to sleep with me?' That idea filled Ophelia with so much rage that she could barely voice the question.

'I wanted you…I still want you,' Lysander stated without a shred of discomfiture. 'That is a separate issue.'

Ophelia shuddered. A separate issue? Who did he think he was kidding? He had set her up for seduction and she had been too stupid to recognise his intentions. It took massive will-power but she managed to ignore his provocative admission. 'Right now we have to concentrate our energy on our differences.'

'In bed.'

'No, *not* in bed!' Ophelia contradicted between gritted teeth of restraint.

'If I agree to sell you the house now, will you sign over the walled garden to me? And forget about us continuing the charade that we are a normal married couple?'

Suddenly serious again, Lysander slid off the bed in a fluid movement. 'No. That's not possible.'

'You could at least *consider* the idea. It's a fair offer. For goodness' sake, why do we have to go on with this stupid pretence? It doesn't make sense.'

His handsome bone structure was taut below his bronzed skin. 'I have excellent reasons that I do not choose to share with you.'

'So that's put me in my place again, has it?' Sizzling with temper and frustration at that snub, Ophelia folded her arms with a jerk.

'Right now your place is by my side.'

'I will not dignify that with an answer! You're being horribly unreasonable.'

'I have an important question,' Lysander countered levelly. 'Will you allow the restoration work here to continue?'

Ophelia almost uttered a furious negative. Then she thought of the roof leaking and the damage that would continue if she took a selfish short-term view of the situation. She couldn't face doing that to the house she loved. 'Yes!' she ground out between clenched teeth.

Stalking over to the bed, she snatched up a pillow and the bedspread that had spilled onto the floor. She marched over to the luxuriously upholstered ottoman couch by the window.

'Aren't you hungry?' Lysander indicated the selection of food on offer. 'Neither of us had the chance to eat this afternoon.'

In spite of the fact that her tummy was growling with emptiness, Ophelia wrapped herself in the bedspread and lay down on the couch. 'Goodnight.'

Lysander surveyed his defiant bride while he satisfied his appetite. A slight frown line now divided his ebony brows, for she was not behaving as he had expected. She was excessively obstinate. Why had she offered to sell the house without any effort to negotiate a stupendous price? Why the continued obsession with the walled garden? Did she genuinely like getting muddy? Why was she set on being a thorn in his flesh, rather than taking immediate advantage of his need for her continuing presence in his life? What had happened to her profiteering instincts? Cue for diamonds, he decided. It was time to show her the sparkling financial benefits of meeting his expectations. He swept up the phone to organise it.

Five minutes later he strode over to the ottoman, lifted Ophelia off it and strode back to the bed.

'What the blazes do you think you're doing?' she yelled at him.

'You sleep in the same bed,' Lysander informed her, blue-shadowed jaw line set at an obdurate angle of challenge.

Ophelia was taken aback to feel tears threatening because she was genuinely exhausted and the prospect of another rousing battle of wits was too much for her just then. 'Don't you dare touch me,' she warned him.

But it was soon obvious that Lysander had far more important matters in mind than sex. While she lay there with her back rigidly turned to him, he made five separate phone calls in a total of three different languages. His dark deep drawl was brisk and authoritative. But he paced round the room at length on another call, his voice softening in tone as he spoke in

Greek. He even laughed a couple of times, although that humorous note struck her as a little forced. She was convinced he was talking to another woman and she strained to catch every nuance even though she couldn't understand a word. Was he explaining to a favoured mistress why he hadn't mentioned the little fact that he was getting married? Why wasn't he prepared to write off their marriage as a mistake? Why the need for an ongoing pretence?

And why had he slept with her? She couldn't accept that the chemistry was as strong for him as it was for her, because he was a highly sophisticated man with an endless procession of gorgeous women to choose from. He was also extremely clever and a brilliant strategist. When she had tried to deny that they were truly married, he had simply turned the tables on her by sweeping her off to bed.

While Ophelia agonised over her failure to say no, Lysander had a television wheeled in and watched the business news, which provoked another round of phone calls. She was almost begging for mercy by midnight. He hadn't even noticed she had a pillow over her head to blank out the light and noise level. An alpha-male workaholic, he had the most appalling level of energy. He also had a passion for controlling everybody and everything around him. His nature was neither tolerant nor patient. He was the last guy alive who would stand the hassle of coping with a demanding, difficult wife. In that knowledge, Ophelia savoured, lay her salvation and her escape route from the shackles of a marriage she didn't want. What would Lysander most dislike?

Publicity would obviously come top of the list. He liked his privacy, so a wife who gave an interview to a downmarket tabloid would be an embarrassment. And she suspected that a clingy, possessive woman always demanding to know where he was and who he was with would revolt him even more. She would have to be careful not to overdo it, though. A sleepy smile melted the tension from Ophelia's troubled mouth. Being a nightmare wife might well be fun and should ensure that she got back to her garden sooner rather than later.

For the third time the following day, Lysander checked that no phone call or message from Ophelia had been intercepted and withheld from him.

His sardonic mouth compressing into an even thinner line, he turned his attention back to the board meeting. The stock-market crisis had ensured that he had to fly back to London at seven that morning. Unsated desire had sentenced him to a restless night and plunged him into an icy shower at dawn. One tiny taste of Ophelia had unleashed a disturbingly powerful storm of sexual craving. What the hell was the matter with him? He couldn't concentrate and he hated the unfamiliar edgy tension nagging at him.

In contrast, Ophelia, to whom histrionics came naturally, had happily slept in his arms half the night as well as through his departure. But then he was convinced that Ophelia would sleep through an earthquake, since he had contrived to clasp a superb pearl and diamond necklace round her neck without wakening her. Even though he had spoken to her she had only mumbled like a zombie and curled up in a ball again.

Any woman, however, would be overwhelmed by so magnificent a gift, he reasoned with conviction. He had also for the first time in his life left a note explaining his absence. *And* during the course of a phenomenally busy morning he had also arranged for the walled garden to be managed by an experienced horticulturist during their absence. In short, Lysander could not recall when he had ever made that much effort on a woman's behalf and received less appreciation for it. Or, been treated to a total silence that was steadily beginning to grate on him.

Ophelia enjoyed an equally busy morning. She had opened her eyes to a terse five-word unsigned note on the pillow. 'At office, flight Greece 20.00 hrs.' She had almost leapt out of bed and saluted with a 'Yes, sir!' as though she were in the military. That amused response was doused by the staggering discovery that she was wearing an opulent pearl and diamond necklace, which put her worryingly in mind of a very elegant dog collar. Was it payment for her virginity? A reward for submission?

Filled with self-loathing at that awful suspicion, Ophelia was sufficiently preoccupied to find herself accepting the luxury of breakfast in bed without complaint. The same maid offered to run her a bath and lay out her clothes and a PA phoned to tell her that she would be leaving for Lysander's house in London at eleven. Ophelia, who had relished her recent freedom to work all the hours of daylight in her garden, felt trapped by the schedule already mapped out for her.

Ophelia rang Pamela.

'No, of course I didn't tell my brother about your marriage,' Pamela declared. 'In fact Matt's furious that I didn't tip him off. I'm practically under siege by the paparazzi down here. Lysander's security men have put up barriers at the foot of the lane and the police are patrolling. It's hugely exciting.'

Ophelia was deep in thought. 'Do you think anyone would be interested in interviewing me?'

'Are you crazy? Any journalist would kill for the chance! You're hot news now.'

Ophelia reckoned that she would never have a better opportunity to take the first step in her campaign to regain her freedom. Did she have the nerve to pull it off? She could not think of anything that Lysander would like less than a wife who could not wait to gush about him and his lifestyle in print. 'I think it would be fun to do an interview, but it would have to be in London this afternoon. Do you think your brother would like to do it?'

Pamela was so thrilled by that offer that she offered to act as a go-between and handed out loads of tips on self-presentation. Ophelia inspected her new wardrobe with a purposeful glint in her gaze and combined several colourful items to achieve the tarty over-the-top effect she wanted. Lysander had to be made to appreciate that threat could only take him so far and no further, and that it would provide no defence whatsoever against the indignity of an unsuitable wife.

Lysander travelled back to his London town house around four that afternoon and found it in uproar. Stamitos greeted him tensely at the door and informed him that Ophelia was giving an interview to the press. Staff were grouped in doorways in strained silence. Nobody had the courage to meet Lysander's utterly disbelieving gaze.

'Which newspaper?' Lysander demanded, thinking some sixth-sense prompting must have urged him home a good five hours in advance of his usual finishing time.

Stamitos's big shoulders took on a visible slump. He named a very popular tabloid that had run several scurrilous stories about Lysander's sex life in recent years. For a split second Lysander actually felt his skin turn clammy with shock, a sensation he had experienced on only one other occasion since reaching adulthood, which had been when his mother's illness was first diagnosed.

'Where are they?'

'The library,' Stamitos said heavily.

Lysander could barely credit what he was being told. *His* library, the most private place in his London home, into which he invited only a chosen few. He had failed to appreciate that the very fact that Ophelia was his wife had put her in a position of unfettered power. Who would dare to question anything she did unless he first told them to do so? But why the hell hadn't someone had the courage to phone him and let him know what was happening?

The library door stood open on a room crowded with people and camera equipment. Lysander breathed in slow and deep. It was beneath his dignity to make a scene but the violation of his privacy felt like an act of treachery. Ophelia was curled up on an antique sofa, looking as tiny, exotic and colourful as a tropical bird. Her make-up was dramatic and she had teamed a very short cerise pink dress with over-the-knee sheer black lace stockings and silver high heels. It was a bizarre outfit. His attention travelled from her enormous lilac-shadowed eyes to her glistening cherry-red mouth and lingered with satisfaction on the pearl and diamond necklace before heading down over the pouting swell of her breasts and finishing at the slender expanse of white thigh visible above the lace stocking. His libido reacted with raunchy enthusiasm bizarre could be surprisingly sexy.

'Lysander came to see my home and it was love at first sight,' Ophelia was gushing with a huge smile. 'I am so lucky Matt. Right now it feels like I'm living a fairy tale!'

Lysander stared at that wide natural smile, noting that he

had never seen it before, while wondering if there just might be a seed of truth in that brash declaration. All too many women had gone overboard for Lysander, which was why he preferred casual relationships. Constantly arguing with him could be Ophelia's way of hiding her feelings or even a perverse way of attempting to grab and hold his attention. Was that why she had invited the media into his home and was talking like an overexcited schoolgirl? Some people would do virtually anything to get publicity. Was this simply the fifteen minutes of fame that she felt she had to have? And why did she sound so chummy with the interviewer?

Lysander watched the young male journalist ogle Ophelia's legs as she shifted position and suddenly it annoyed the hell out of Lysander that his wife was wearing a short skirt.

'I want that smile of hers for the front cover,' the cameraman was telling his assistant.

'How does it feel to be married to a billionaire?'

'Blissful.' Ophelia touched the magnificent jewels encircling her white throat with reverent fingertips. 'Lysander gave me this necklace today.'

Lysander set his even white teeth together and ground them. Didn't she realise what she sounded like? He wanted to gag her for her own protection.

'I understand that even though you only got married yesterday your husband is already back at work. How do you feel about that?'

'Like I've been abandoned,' Ophelia declared earnestly. 'Lysander will have to change his lifestyle. I believe married couples should spend a lot of time together. I plan on going everywhere with Lysander. His friends will be my friends and I will share all his interests—'

'Is that because you doubt your husband's ability to stay faithful if you're not around?'

'Oh, I don't doubt that at all,' Ophelia told him chirpily. 'Lysander worships the ground I walk on. I know he's missing me just as much as I'm missing him today.'

At that precise moment, Ophelia saw Lysander and a guilty blush of mortification enveloped her in a heat wave from head to toe. Yet, for a split second, she still stared for he looked breathtakingly handsome and the sexy epitome of sleek male sophistication. Unfortunately she had not expected him to show up during the actual interview when giant fibs and breezy inanities of the most embarrassing sort were tripping off her tongue. Heads began turning and silence fell as his presence registered on Pamela's brother, Matt, and his companions.

'Which is why I came home early,' Lysander drawled with a glittering smile, crossing the room to close an arm round his blushing bride.

Ophelia was struck dumb, but it didn't matter because Lysander took over with a witty male quip about some racing event that had taken place that day. And suddenly, all the men were talking cars and drivers and she was no longer the centre of attention. In the midst of it, Lysander gave her a gentle little push in the direction of the door. 'Go upstairs,' he breathed in a don't-mess-with-me undertone before he concluded the interview session with the information that she had to get ready for their flight.

Ophelia had barely reached the bedroom when Lysander strode through the door in her wake. She spun round, nervous as a cat, convinced he would be furious and, even though that was the result she had sought, she wasn't looking forward to the fallout.

'There are three little things you need to learn to survive the next five minutes,' Lysander imparted huskily.

'And what are they?' Taut with uncertainty, Ophelia connected with his scorching bronze gaze and felt dizzy. Indeed she felt the sexual power of that driving appraisal to the very core of her being. Her breasts stirred within the push-up bra she wore, the delicate peaks tingling into rigid points. A white-hot tension clenched between her thighs, making her embarrassingly aware of the melting warmth there.

'One. You don't talk to the press in any shape or form unless I authorise it—and I never will. As I didn't tell you that, I will not hold it against you on this one occasion. Who was the journalist? He was too familiar with you.'

'Pamela's brother, Matt.' Ophelia watched his lean, powerful face darken with disapproval. 'You think he was to blame for leaking the news of our marriage to the media but he had nothing to do with it. Pamela didn't tell him or anybody else. You condemned my best friend unfairly.'

Lysander made no response.

Deflated by that non-reaction, Ophelia tilted her chin. 'So because of that, I decided that if I was going to give anyone an interview it should be Matt Arnold.'

Lysander jerked loose his tie and unbuttoned his collar. 'Two,' he continued, ignoring her protest in defence of her friend. 'You do not appear in public in clothes that reveal that much of your body.'

Ophelia was bewildered by that charge, as she had not thought a glimpse of cleavage and a little leg would bother him in the slightest. Her outfit was tame in comparison with those worn by most female celebrities.

'I'm wearing underwear,' she told him with a sniff, well

primed by Pamela's addiction to magazines to know that some women chose not to do so.

In the act of removing his jacket, Lysander gave her a smouldering look of censure. 'Don't even think about going out without it. In fact everything between shoulder and knee should be out of sight.'

'Is that a fact? So why is it that according to what I've been told you're always being seen out with half-naked women?'

'Don't be foolish,' Lysander drawled with hauteur. 'You're my wife and in a different league. I expect modest and circumspect behaviour from you.'

Ophelia was dumbfounded by that little speech, which fairly bulged with the hypocrisy of double standards, but which carried not a single note of apology or self-justification. But she was also amazed that he wasn't shouting at her. 'So what was the third thing I needed to learn to survive the next five minutes?'

'How to appease an angry husband.' Lysander strolled forward and scooped her up in his arms.

A startled gasp escaped her as he hoisted her up onto the bed. Stunning metallic eyes blazed over her and he ravished her mouth with a hard, hungry kiss that sent her blood racing through her veins. The stab of his tongue mimicked the carnal thrust of his lean body and left her shaking with excitement, a knot of heat and tension pulsing and tightening low in her pelvis.

A wolfish smile on his lean powerful features, he kneed apart her legs and skimmed exploring fingers up below her skirt. It was broad daylight. She was shocked, uncertain. She knew she should stop him. She knew that she had promised herself that she would not sleep with him again but he was touching her with an intimacy that left her boneless with desire. He pushed up her skirt.

'No, we shouldn't,' she mumbled in desperation.

'But you're so ready for me.' Knowing fingertips traced the damp, swollen heart of her beneath the satin panties she wore and when he found the most sensitive spot of all, she moaned in supplication. As she writhed he made a roughened sound of masculine appreciation. Shame that she couldn't control or hide her eagerness slivered through her.

Lysander studied her with smouldering satisfaction. 'When all those guys were looking at your dainty white thighs, *this* is what I was thinking about, *yineka mou*.' he confessed. 'My right to lie between them.'

He tugged off her panties, positioned her to his liking and mounted her without ceremony. She trembled when she felt the hot probe of his rigid shaft against her yielding softness. He plunged into her honeyed passage hard and fast. It was primitive, raw and unbelievably exciting. Shock waves of erotic sensation racked her slender body. Raising her to him, he sank even deeper into her lush depths, withdrew and then slammed back into her. Delirious with need and on fire with sensation, she cried out. The pleasure was wildly intense. His rampant passion sent her soaring to a mindless peak of ecstasy where the world shattered around her. Nothing had ever felt so powerful and her slender body convulsed in wild contractions of delight. Drained in the aftermath and shaken by the sense of connection she now had with him, she wrapped her arms round him and struggled to breathe again.

Lysander was stunned to appreciate that he had lost control with her. Questioning eyes screened by his thick lashes, Lysander gazed down at her and marvelled at his appetite for her. 'Did I hurt you?'

'No,' she framed gruffly, mortified by what had just happened between them and twisting her head away.

'I was rough and you're tiny, *yineka mou*.' His dark drawl hoarse, he bent his handsome head and pressed his sensual mouth to the tender skin of her throat.

'Hmm…' Tiny little shivers rippled through Ophelia in response. She was sensitised to his every caress.

'I'm a very sexual man. You excite me,' he confided huskily, grazing her delicate skin with his teeth. 'But I don't think you could take me again right now.'

When she realized that she was being asked a question, Ophelia's face flamed. Even lying there she was conscious of the ache of discomfort his passion had induced. 'No, I couldn't,' she agreed in stifled embarrassment.

'My little virgin wife—I should have been more considerate.' His tone was teasing as he levered back from her, adjusted his clothing and smoothed back his black hair. He looked cool and in control. Yet after that wild conflagration, Ophelia honestly thought that she would never be the same again. With shaking hands she yanked down her skirt over her nakedness.

Without warning a frown line divided his well-shaped brows. 'Are you using any contraception?'

In a daze at that query, Ophelia shook her head and sat up.

Lysander had fallen very still and there was an ashen quality to his skin, for he was shattered by his carelessness and unable to explain it even to his own satisfaction. The very last thing he wanted was a child. As he had no desire to be a father, he had always been very careful not to run any risks in that department. If his caution had occasionally restricted his enjoyment he had accepted that.

'*Theos*…I'm afraid that I didn't take any precautions

either,' Lysander imparted with a gravity that made his feelings on the subject very clear. 'I won't attempt to excuse my negligence. It's not a mistake I've made before and I hope that there won't be any repercussions.'

Ophelia dropped her head and very much hoped so too because his attitude chilled her. He was appalled by the very idea that she might fall pregnant. Negligence was a serious word to use. She was frantically counting dates inside her head and stiffened at the acknowledgement that she was dangerously within reach of the most fertile part of her cycle. 'Let's hope for the best,' she muttered stiltedly.

'I have some calls to make before we head for the airport.'

Ophelia let him get as far as the door before she spoke again. 'Did you believe me about Matt Arnold? That his sister, Pamela, didn't leak the fact that we were married to the newspapers?'

Sardonic eyes rested on her anxious face. 'Of course I didn't believe you. How could I? Perhaps you leaked that story yourself. Your conduct today underlined your guilt.'

'And how on earth do you make that out?' Ophelia snapped in disconcertion.

Lysander dealt her a derisive look of disbelief. 'You married me yesterday. Today you invited a newspaper into my home. Your eagerness for media attention speaks for itself.'

Ophelia went for a shower in the state-of-the-art bathroom and while she washed she cried with anger, frustration and the most awful hollow sense of homesickness. It should have occurred to her that he would make that rather obvious deduction. An exercise intended merely to annoy him had rebounded on her, for she knew he would never accept now that she had not tipped off the press about their wedding. He saw her as a cheap publicity-hungry trollop, fine for sex but nothing else.

So why did that bother her so much when all she wanted from him was a divorce? Although how did she dare to ask herself such a question when he had put her on his bed and she had demonstrated as much self-command as a rag doll in the passionate encounter that had followed? When she looked at him, she burned for him and all her defences crumbled. It was that basic and it was the most tormenting truth she had ever had to deal with. She had believed that she was strong but now she was confronting her weakness and her pride was in the dust.

But why *was* she so hurt? That was what scared her the most. Why did she feel so rejected? Naturally he didn't want her to conceive, but had he had to turn pale as death at what was surely only a small risk? She didn't want a baby either, of course she didn't—well, at some time maybe in the future with the right person, and Lysander Metaxis was most decidedly not the right person. Her hunger for him had nothing to do with feelings, she reasoned fiercely. It was disgusting that it should be that way and she was ashamed of it, but she was not remotely like her mother. No, she wasn't, she absolutely wasn't. She was too intelligent to get fixated on a man who would never love her, who would never offer her exclusive affection or fidelity and who would never want to walk down the street with her and show her off. Much, much too intelligent…

CHAPTER SEVEN

It was late afternoon the following day before Lysander and Ophelia finally landed in Greece.

A late seasonal fall of snow the night before had led to a cessation of flights and long delays. Hiring accommodation at an airport hotel, Lysander used the extra time to work with his business team and ensured that Ophelia didn't get the chance to talk to him in private again. Indeed, faced with his cool detachment, she felt like the invisible woman. Listening to dialogues that centred solely on the stock market, derivatives and interest rates did not improve her mood. Once or twice, when she looked at Lysander, she found herself helplessly reliving the raw heat of their lovemaking the previous afternoon; his aloofness since then could only make her feel furiously ashamed of that episode. In the early hours she took a nap in the bedroom of their suite while still fully clothed.

Overlooked in the excitement of the stock market opening, she was the last person to be roused and she missed out on breakfast and the chance to change out of her creased clothing, so had to take care of that necessity when they finally boarded the jet. By then she was in a defiant mood and, disdaining the more dressy options in her suitcase, she pulled on casual combats and a T-shirt. Lysander had insisted that they pretend that their marriage was normal. He had threatened her with court action, then had wrenched her from her home, her garden and her parrot while persistently refusing to offer her the smallest explanation for his behaviour. But when was *he* planning to start acting like a newly married man? Or were his staff already aware that his marriage was an empty charade? Albeit a charade with a little sexual action thrown in for colour, Ophelia reflected, squirming with self-loathing.

When she emerged from the luxurious cabin an odd little silence fell and absolutely nobody looked in her direction, while her husband's attention seemed welded to his newspaper. It was a response that did nothing to relieve her suspicion that on board a Metaxis jet non-working personnel ranked as the lowest of the low in the pecking order.

Lysander, however, was gripped by the article on his bride in the newspaper for which Matt, Pamela Arnold's brother, was a writer. Unfortunately the old link between the Metaxis and Stewart families—the wedding that never took place between Aristide and Cathy—had been dug up and given a fresh melodramatic airing. Lysander hoped his mother didn't come across the item, since she tended to be sensitive about that episode and he was determined to keep her spirits up during her medical treatment.

Ophelia's interview was only the jewel in the crown of a spread that contrived to flatter her from every possible angle. The dialogue had been polished clean of the smallest hint that Ophelia might regard gifts of very expensive jewellery as the best bit of having married a billionaire. Indeed in the published version Ophelia now waxed lyrical about how she hoped to use her privileged position to do some good in the world and came across as a thoroughly nice girl with traditional values.

He was very surprised to learn that until the age of sixteen years she had lived in a tough housing estate with a mother who had problems with alcohol and unsuitable men. Social Services had been frequent callers. There was a photograph of Ophelia about the age of ten clutching a dark-haired toddler. They looked like half-starved waifs.

'Ophelia was a great little mother to her sister. Took her to school, did everything for her, but then she didn't have a choice, did she?' a former neighbour was quoted as saying. 'Her ma, Cathy, was more of a child than she was.'

Lysander wondered if the little sister had died with the mother in the train crash as there was no further mention of her. Without doubt, as sob stories went, it was a blinder and the unnamed contributors must all have been close friends, for nobody had a bad word to say about his bride. Had her difficult childhood made her avaricious? Or had her troubled mother and scheming, embittered grandmother tainted her with a desire for revenge?

Why did nothing about Ophelia add up? Why was she such a mixture of opposing traits? She had trained for three years to be a low-earning horticulturist and there was a picture of her dressed like a scarecrow—albeit one with shining eyes and a happy smile. Yes, she liked getting muddy and clearly always had. He found it hard to equate that Ophelia with the woman who had posed in lace stockings and with a vacuous smile for the camera. Why had she claimed to want out of their marriage when, just twenty-four hours later, she had done her utmost to attract the very worst kind of publicity?

When Lysander handed Ophelia a newspaper she felt

bewildered—until she saw the picture of herself and Molly. Her tummy went into a nervous spiral, a reaction that only got worse as she ploughed through the article that laid bare her chequered childhood. Her late mother's inadequacy as a parent was now revealed for all to see and it filled Ophelia with shame. But what she hated most was the raking over of Cathy's doomed romance with Aristide Metaxis and she blamed herself for being stupid enough to court publicity in the first place. A lesson had been learned, she conceded painfully.

'I'm afraid I have some matters to take care of before I can join you on the island,' Lysander murmured as they disembarked the plane.

'*What* island?' Ophelia enquired stiffly without looking at him.

Even Lysander's tough hide was pierced by the ramifications of that leading question. 'I bought an island a few years ago.'

Her expression stony and unimpressed, Ophelia pursed her pink lips as if she were sucking on a lemon. 'I suppose it's surrounded by sea and very private?'

'*Ne*…Yes.'

'How thrilling,' Ophelia droned in a not-thrilled voice, imagining herself marooned on a giant sun-baked rock without occupation while he enjoyed himself elsewhere. 'Please don't worry about me. I may well be as dried-up as an Egyptian mummy by the time you deign to take notice of my existence again. But no doubt if someone props me up in a corner you'll be quite happy with the remains rather than the demanding reality of a living, breathing wife!'

'Very funny,' Lysander countered flatly.

'You ignored me all the way here—you didn't even tell me where we were going—'

'We *are* in the middle of a stock-market crisis,' Lysander growled in an incredulous undertone. 'While *you* were sleeping, *I* was working!'

Shimmering eyes the colour of pale blue ice landed on him. '*So?*' Ophelia challenged just as a plethora of cameras went off behind security barriers in the airport arrivals hall that prevented the paparazzi from getting any closer to their quarries.

Wholly disconcerted by a counter-attack of a type he had never previously received, because the importance of making money had always provided an acceptable catch-all excuse, Lysander gritted his perfect teeth. 'Smile for the cameras,' he told her in a sardonic undertone.

'Oh, dear, my battery's gone flat,' Ophelia responded. 'Nothing to smile about either—'

'You're the one who set off this media circus!'

Ophelia paled at that blunt reminder and contrived a rather hunted curve of the lips. In truth she was genuinely shocked when it finally dawned on her that the heaving crush of shouting people behind the barriers was composed of members of the press waiting solely on their arrival.

In the limousine, Lysander turned bronzed eyes of censure on her. 'I expect you to behave in public!'

'I expect you to behave in private,' Ophelia responded with spirit. 'You told me to act like a wife and that's what you're getting. No bride in her right mind would put up with this kind of treatment on what is supposed to be her honeymoon!'

Lysander startled her by throwing back his arrogant dark head and laughing with husky appreciation. She was crazy, but it exerted the strangest appeal for him. Just as quickly he remembered the silk and velvet feel of her and the eager curve and welcome of her slight body against his. The heavy pulse at his groin threatened to become painful. He closed his lean, powerful hands over hers and pulled her to him with easy strength. 'If I make it back tonight, I promise not to ignore you,' he murmured huskily, slumberous metallic eyes full of sensual promise.

Her rising temper was punctured by the shock of that unsettlingly direct masculine response as it made nonsense of her attempt to call him to book and shame him for his attitude. Ophelia went red to the roots of her hair. 'That isn't what I meant,' she hissed. 'You are not welcome in *my* bed. There's not going to be any more of that kind of nonsense—'

In silent answer, Lysander clamped her up against the hard contours of his lean, muscular frame and ravished her soft mouth with devouring hunger. A glittering ripple of white-hot heat and energy snaked through her and she fought a pitched battle with her response before the sudden sound of the passenger door opening made both of them pull apart in a simultaneous action.

'Later, *yineka mou*,' he breathed, before he climbed out in front of a large building. The passenger door thudded shut again and the limo moved off.

In a daze Ophelia shook her head, uncertain whether he was finally acting the part of her new husband or simply set on outmanoeuvring her.

Inside the exclusive clinic, Lysander was greeted by the medical specialist he had arranged to meet. Reassured by the latest bulletin on his mother's health, he used a private lift to access her comfortable suite. The older woman's passion for keeping her illness a secret from all but her closest friends had exasperated him. But he was deeply attached to Virginia and, although it was not a sentiment he could bring himself to share even with her, he tried to respect her wishes. Her cancer diagnosis had shattered him and the strain of keeping his concern hidden had been compounded when the older woman initially succumbed to depression and refused to consider surgery.

Although exhausted by her recent treatment, Virginia, a slim woman in her late fifties, still maintained the highest standards of grooming. But her son was quick to notice her reddened eyelids. He also recognised the corner of the newspaper protruding from beneath a hastily rearranged bedspread.

'You've already seen the article about Ophelia,' he guessed.

'I get all the English newspapers.'

'It upset you.'

Her discomfort patent, Virginia evaded his gaze. 'No, memories of the past did that. Naturally I'm curious about my new daughter-in-law—her mother was once my friend.'

'If you had agreed to my telling Ophelia that you were in hospital, I would've brought her to meet you.' In truth, however, Lysander was not yet sure that he could trust Ophelia with his vulnerable mother. Virginia would always be the woman who had supplanted Cathy Stewart in Aristide's affections.

'I refuse to blight your first weeks together with this illness,' the older woman declared staunchly. 'Particularly so soon after your wife has lost her grandmother. You shouldn't even be here tonight; you should be with your bride.'

An indulgent look on his lean, strong face, Lysander sat down. 'I haven't seen you for several days.'

Virginia sighed. 'But I'm content. I was very happy when you told me you'd got married. I *swear*, I was only scared for about twenty seconds thinking that you might've married the poor girl purely to get hold of Madrigal Court!'

With difficulty he retained his charismatic smile. 'Where would you get such a wild idea from?'

'You're my son and I love you, even though you can be very ruthless,' his mother retorted. 'But I know you would only give up your freedom for someone very special and that quiet, quick wedding was very much your style. From what I've read, though, Ophelia's had rather an unhappy life to date—'

'But she doesn't wear it like a badge. She sparkles.' Lysander selected the descriptive word with care, thinking of the sassy light in Ophelia's eyes and the liveliness of her quick movements.

Virginia rested anxious brown eyes on her handsome son. 'What I'm about to say may annoy you, but if I don't say it and your marriage ends in divorce, I'll blame myself. You must've been angry about the interview that Ophelia gave to the press. She needs time and support to adjust to our world—'

'Of course.'

'Too many women have spoiled you, or perhaps I should say that the possession of power has spoiled you,' the older woman murmured heavily. 'You haven't had to learn how to compromise. I want your marriage to work. I need to know that you have a loving home and family to rely on.'

Lysander paled and drew in a stark swift breath. *If your marriage ends in divorce, I'll blame myself.* That assurance in tandem with that word, 'family', struck him like a thunderclap. Virginia must always have been eager for him to settle down with one woman. Respect for his privacy had kept her silent until illness had concentrated her thoughts on a future that she feared she might not be around to share. He should have guessed that his mother was secretly longing for him to present her with a grandchild. Even though he was an adult, more toughened than most by his experience of violence, betrayal and cruelty, Virginia continued to worry incessantly about his happiness rather than her own. More moved than he could bear, he sprang up and walked over to the window.

'Cherish Ophelia—don't let business become an excuse to neglect her. There, all done,' Virginia muttered tightly, well aware that she had trespassed where angels feared to tread. 'I promise that I won't say another embarrassing word.'

But though Virginia moved on to urge him to tell her about how her childhood home had fared in Gladys Stewart's hands, Lysander remained disconcerted by what she had said to him. Such interference in his private life was unprecedented and tapped into the concern he contrived to suppress most of the time. Now that concern resurfaced and a hollow sensation filled him. Did his mother know something about her medical condition that he did not? Although her treatment was proceeding well, did she have reason to suspect that her long-term prognosis was poor?

Her first glimpse of Lysander's island took Ophelia's breath away; Kastros was very lush and beautiful.

A colourful fishing village lay at one end of the island while Lysander's stunning contemporary house sat in splendid isolation at the other, the two joined by a winding single ribbon of road. His home overlooked a glorious bay bounded by pine forests and a shimmering white crescent of empty sand. When Ophelia walked through the front door, she was greeted by a smiling group of staff, who could not do enough for her. She was offered an immediate tour of the vast house, which was amazing in terms of design, technology and comfort. A delicious dinner was served on a shaded terrace.

The chef even came out to check that she had enjoyed the food. She was impressed to death—she couldn't help it.

But as the night hours advanced and there was no further word from Lysander, a closer scrutiny of her surroundings had a rather different effect on her. The master bedroom suite was built on palatial lines. She was astonished when she discovered that the closets in the dressing room already contained a remarkable array of brand-new designer garments, sets of silk lingerie and accessories—all in a selection of sizes. The adjoining bathroom was stuffed to the gills with a wide selection of exclusive perfume and cosmetics. Slowly it dawned on Ophelia that the house was a playboy's paradise where Lysander must have entertained many different women.

She rested newly aware and censorious eyes on the massive bed, the number of mirrors and the mood lighting. His bedroom was a sophisticated adult pleasure room. No prizes for guessing how Lysander liked to relax between business deals! With lots of sex and the sort of women who expected to be richly remunerated for their time in a billionaire's bed. She thought of the necklace he had given her and shuddered with distaste.

By midnight, Ophelia had installed her possessions in a guest room at the far end of the house. She had to make boundaries and stick to them. Besides, she wanted a divorce and her goal was to become a thorn in Lysander's flesh. Her good behaviour had not advanced her cause at the airport hotel or during the flight to Greece. Lysander was accustomed to women who accepted being treated like the wallpaper. She should have moaned incessantly and clung to him, but she had shrunk from putting on such an act in front of his staff.

Her pride revolted at the suspicion that she was already

allowing Lysander to ride roughshod over her. He had torn her from her busy, fulfilling life and dumped her on a private island where she had neither company nor occupation. And where was he? That was what Ophelia wanted to know. While she was marooned in a giant house in the middle of nowhere, where was her bridegroom and what was *he* doing? After all, hadn't he insisted that they pretend that theirs was a normal marriage? Was every single sacrifice to be hers?

Mid-morning the next day, she was informed of Lysander's imminent arrival long before she actually saw the helicopter flying in over the bay. The staff rushed around. Anticipation hung heavy in the air. Everywhere Lysander went, the red carpet was rolled out to welcome him and awe-inspired ordinary mortals made enormous efforts to ensure that nothing displeased him. She discovered that it took considerable courage to ignore the fuss and the expectation that she behave in a similar fashion.

Lysander was annoyed that Ophelia wasn't in the front hall when he arrived. He discovered that he had a surprisingly clear concept of how a wife should behave. Ophelia should have been eager to see him and have taken the first opportunity to greet him. Didn't she know anything at all about what pleased a man? Well, not in the bedroom, he conceded, but he didn't have a problem with his role of instructor in that department. Virginia's strictures nudged to the forefront of his mind and his sleek black brows pleated. Of course, if he didn't tell Ophelia what he expected from her how was she to know? Perhaps he should write it all down in clear, concise language that could not be misunderstood. Proper guidelines would soon sort out the problem.

'Where is my wife?' he demanded of his staff.

Lysander could not credit the answer. Broad shoulders straight as axe handles, the carriage of his big powerful frame imposing, he strode through his house and knocked on the relevant guest room door. A man spoiled by too many women or the possession of too much power might not have knocked, might even have raised his voice from the foot of the corridor. But he was *not* such a man, Lysander told himself with sterling conviction.

On the other side of the door, Ophelia tensed and braced herself for a showdown.

CHAPTER EIGHT

'YES?' Ophelia enquired frostily as the door spread back in an ever-widening arc. It was a challenge not to react physically to her sudden view of Lysander, for the minute she saw him she became intensely aware of him. It wasn't just that he was gorgeous and intensely, unashamedly masculine. It wasn't even his vibrant aura of energy that attracted her most. It was the powerful buzz of his presence that excited her to the point that she literally held her breath.

Dense black lashes semi-screened Lysander's stunning bronze gaze and a wicked smile of amusement marked his stubborn, passionate mouth. She might not have been poised by the front door, but she had most definitely been waiting for him. Her crystalline blue eyes glimmered like stars in her heart-shaped face. Her tension and unease were so palpable in the delicate contours of her face and the tautness of her slight figure that his exasperation evaporated. He strode forward and snatched her up into his arms with raw masculine enthusiasm.

'*Sta diavolo*…I thought I was never going to get here, *yineka mou*!'

'Lysander!' she squeaked and it wasn't supposed to be a

squeak, it was supposed to be a freezing reproof. But once again he had taken her totally by surprise and had steamrollered over her defences before she could muster a more forbidding stance.

'I haven't tasted you since the day before yesterday,' Lysander declared thickly against the tremulous line of her mouth. Then, pulling her right into him, he strode with her out of the room, both arms wrapped round her in a potent embrace. 'For a man of my strong appetites that is a very long time, *hara mou*.'

His deep accented drawl shimmied down her taut spine like a velvet caress.

'P-put me down,' Ophelia stammered in a hoarse undertone.

'You don't mean that, not now that you finally have me all to yourself. I will never ignore your existence again,' Lysander husked, letting his white teeth nibble at her lower lip and taking advantage of her strangled gasp to dip his tongue into the moist tender interior of her mouth, which she had attempted to deny him.

Her slim fingers clenched the springy depths of his black hair. He used his tongue to dart and thrust with erotic mastery and she shivered violently in his hold. Her body was awakening in a feverish burst of response that was so powerful it almost hurt. She tried to think, to reason, at virtually the same moment that he pushed her flat on a yielding surface. Her heart was pounding fit to burst. He thrust her green cotton top out of his way and dealt even more expeditiously with the wisp of silk and lace that covered the pouting mounds of her breasts as they rose and fell with the rapidity of her breathing.

Stunned by the speed with which events were unfolding and the humming urgency of her own quivering body, Ophelia froze. Her brain might not feel that agile, but the baring of her skin for Lysander's touch sent her mental alarm bells jangling and she whipped up her hands to cover herself. 'I mustn't…' she told him.

'And I must,' Lysander traded with amusement, bending his arrogant dark head to taste her full pink mouth with slow, delicious intensity.

The shimmer of desire washing through her taut length became a hot greedy surge that centred on the pulse at the damp, hot heart of her body. She dug her hips into the mattress in an unconscious need to ease that ache while her palms dropped away from her chest.

'Do that again,' she heard herself whisper.

And he did. Somewhere in the back of her mind she recognised the faint heady aroma of a fragrance that was familiar to her. Her bewildered senses and preoccupied brain attempted to cut through the confused feeling that something didn't fit. He closed his hands over hers to lift her back against the pillows.

Eyes brilliant with hunger, he paused to admire the jutting fullness of her bare breasts. 'Delectable,' he purred, skimming a thumb over a rigid rosy nipple so that her teeth clenched together in helpless reaction.

Her eyes were shut tight. He lowered his head and captured the lush, tender peak with his mouth and his fingers. In the same instant that she clutched at his shoulder to steady herself and her wanton body was racked by an explosion of excruciating pleasure, she recognised the mysterious scent that had tugged at her memory and almost simultaneously appreciated why it had felt *so* wrong. It was a woman's perfume, not a man's cologne.

'You've been with someone else…' Ophelia framed, sick and empty with shock as she made that obvious deduction.

Lysander straightened with a frown. 'What did you say?'

Ophelia wrenched down her top with shaking hands and scrambled clumsily off the bed. Both responses were instinctive. Her skin felt cold and clammy. How could she have been so stupid? She spread a stricken glance round the room, which she had earlier deemed an adult playroom for a man who preferred sexual variety to steady relationships. Well, she could not say that she had not been warned.

'What's wrong?' Lean, strong face taut, Lysander was studying her with concerned bronze eyes.

Ophelia folded her arms because she was afraid he would see that she was shaking. Her legs were all woolly and wobbly. She felt utterly betrayed and foolish. 'That's why you stayed in Athens last night. You were with another woman.'

Lysander had fallen still. He had no idea what had sparked off the accusation and he had no intention of responding to it. He had a policy of never explaining or denying such allegations and it had served him well since the teen years. He didn't do jealous scenes. He didn't soothe tantrums. He didn't go there at all.

'Don't you dare stand there looking at me like I've lost my wits!' Ophelia slung at him, her temper rising as her nervous tension ran off the scale.

'What do you expect?' Lysander enquired with abrasive cool. 'One minute we're making love and the next you call a halt without warning and start trying to stage an argument.'

Her indignation was increasing in direct proportion to his cold-blooded lack of concern. 'You've got about as much feeling inside you as the rocks on the beach!'

'But you have more than enough for both of us, *glikia mou*,' Lysander countered, smooth as silk in his satire.

That retaliation struck Ophelia like a sobering slap. He could not have made it clearer that he didn't care how she felt. How could she have slept with a guy willing to treat her like this? A hurricane of stormy emotion clawed at her. On some level she suspected that if she paused for thought and actually faced what she was feeling it might destroy her. She had ignored her misgivings, turned her back on what she knew to be right and succumbed to the temptation he offered. So if she couldn't resist Lysander, did that make her one bit better than the women who couldn't resist him or his wealth?

'Your jacket smells of a woman's perfume,' Ophelia told him resolutely. She was giving him one more chance to explain himself without knowing when she had made the decision to give him an extra opportunity, which he most certainly did not deserve.

Handsome head at an imperious angle, dark, deep-set gaze stony, Lysander lifted and dropped a shoulder in a fluid shrug that just roared bone-deep stubborn insolence. 'I don't do scenes like this.'

All fired up and desperate to hear him assure her that her suspicions were wildly off beam, Ophelia could not believe that that was all he was prepared to offer her in the way of explanation. 'You don't *do*—?'

'I don't accept being shouted at either,' Lysander delivered icily.

'If you imagine that that was a shout, I wouldn't like to think how you would react to the genuine article.' Flushed and rigid, Ophelia rested defiant blue eyes on him and tilted her chin. She would have no peace of mind until she knew the worst and had never ducked bad news in her life. 'Were you with someone else last night? I have the right to know.'

Lysander dealt her a smouldering appraisal. 'You have the right to nothing.'

Her slender hands snapped into tight fists by her side. 'Oh, yes, I do. We're married. If you'd kept it platonic and everything was fake, then I wouldn't have the right to question you like this. But you wouldn't settle for that arrangement,' she reminded him fiercely. 'So, either this is a marriage or it isn't. You can't have it both ways.'

'No comment.'

It was the last straw for Ophelia. She lifted the water carafe by the bed and chucked it at him. She didn't think about doing it, she simply closed her hand round the glass bottle and slung it with all her might. He ducked, which infuriated her, and the glass smashed against the wall, sending pieces of glass and drops of water flying in all directions.

'I need a shower,' Lysander imparted with hauteur. 'Hopefully you'll have calmed down by the time I reappear, *yineka mou.*'

'Don't hold your breath,' Ophelia advised shakily.

In the smouldering silence, Lysander removed his jacket and tossed it on the bed. He was furious with her. How dared she start ranting and raving and throwing things at him? He couldn't believe it, but he had married a bunny-boiler! He would have dumped her if he weren't married to her. Although he wouldn't have dumped her until she had apologised. No, he thought with seething fury, not until he had her in his bed begging for release or on her knees pleading for forgiveness.

'These rooms say all there is to know about your attitude to women,' Ophelia condemned in a driven rush of pent-up feeling. 'You just use us with contempt.'

Lysander swung round. Metallic eyes landed on her like lightning rods. 'What is that supposed to mean?'

'The designer clothes in multi-sizes in the wardrobes. Payment for services received?' she questioned in a voice that was very close to breaking, stark strain etched in her fragile bone structure. 'You don't treat women like equals. You keep them at a distance. You prefer to buy sex or should I call it…rewarding your lovers with very expensive presents?'

Lysander was incensed by that indictment of his character. 'The rich are expected to be generous. I like my guests to enjoy themselves. I won't apologise for that.'

Ophelia compressed her lips. 'I—'

'Be careful how you refer to my sexual partners when you're one of them and when you've cost me much more than any other woman in the short time I've known you,' Lysander drawled in sardonic continuance.

His derision was unconcealed. Ophelia was frozen to the spot by the mortifying truth of his retort. The angry colour bled out from beneath her complexion. 'Neither a borrower nor a lender be' had been one of her grandmother's favourite maxims, because once those lines were blurred obligations were formed. And Ophelia was all too well aware that she had put herself in hock to Lysander through the household bills for Madrigal Court that he'd paid, the repairs he had instigated and also through the clothes and the jewellery he had bought her.

'But I didn't even want to know you, never mind marry you and be stuck out here on your stupid island,' Ophelia whispered tightly, fighting very hard to retain her self-control while rage and tears burned the backs of her eyes. 'Away from my home, from Haddock and my garden…'

'Ripping me off for every penny you can get does entail some sacrifice,' Lysander dropped in with withering cool.

Forced to recall the angry words she had hurled on their wedding day, Ophelia registered that for every action there was a reaction when Lysander was concerned. He hit back hard—and he had just hit back with the hardest blow ever when she'd felt horribly vulnerable. The bathroom door closed. She dived on his jacket and sniffed at the expensive material like a bloodhound. But the elusive scent of the famous designer perfume was unmistakable and could only have been acquired by very close contact.

Her stomach lurching, Ophelia shivered violently. Lysander was perfectly capable of making love to two women in one day. According to Pamela, Lysander's libido was the stuff of legend in the tabloids. She closed her eyes tight. He had had sex with another woman. Stark, unwelcome imagery attacked her imagination. She broke out in a sweat when she found herself inadvertently picturing his lean brown body erotically entwined with a sinuous brunette. In fact she felt so nauseous that she had to sit down and lower her head in an effort to overcome the sickness. Was the woman his mistress? Naturally he wouldn't answer her questions when he was guilty as charged. He wouldn't defend himself, make excuses or apologise or promise that it would never happen again. He believed that he had every right to do as he liked.

So why did she feel as if someone had plunged a skewer through her heart? Why was she shaking all over like an accident victim? Why was there this giant agonised pain inside her? After all, wasn't Lysander behaving exactly as any sane and intelligent woman could have forecast? One woman at a time—fidelity—was not the Metaxis way. She knew that better than anyone. Aristide Metaxis had never restricted himself to a single partner either and growing up with that example within his own home must have made its mark on Lysander, his son.

Ophelia forced herself upright again. It was the wrong moment to get bogged down in analysing emotions that had no bearing whatsoever on her plight. It was practicalities she had to deal with. She was so angry with him for hurting and humiliating her that she was trembling like a leaf. But she was already working out what she had to do to break free, as there was no way that she would allow Lysander to betray her trust. She wondered when money had begun to seem so important to her that she had decided to do wrong in the belief that it would cause no harm and indeed bring about a greater good. The sensible way out of her predicament seemed both clear and simple.

In the room where she had slept the night before, she pulled out a bag and repacked the few items she had brought from home. She ignored the clothes *he* had bought her and even stripped down to her bare skin to discard his fancy underwear. She wanted nothing from him. In fact she wanted nothing more to do with him *ever*.

'Kyria Metaxis…' Stamitos, Lysander's security chief, was crossing the hall when she appeared. 'How may I help you?'

'I'd like to go to the village. I'll drive myself.'

There was a tiny instant of hesitation before Stamitos insisted on carrying her bag for her and personally showed her out to the garage block, which contained an entire line of cars. She was eager to make her departure before Lysander realised that she had gone. She asked if a ferry service to one of the bigger islands ran from the harbour. The older man told her that the ferry would be there early the next morning. The most easily accessible car in the garage was a low black flashy sports model, with a name she didn't recognise. Chucking her bag into the passenger seat with alacrity, Ophelia extended her hand for the keys.

'Let me drive you, Kyria,' Stamitos suggested, looking worried. 'It's a very fast car.'

'I can manage.' Ophelia jumped in, adjusted the seat as best she could and reversed the car like a rally driver.

The afternoon sun was strong in a bright blue sky as the car roared throatily down the road, speeding by lush woods on one side and the sea on the other as it sparkled in the sunlight. She would rent a room in the village for the night. Absorbed in reckoning whether or not she had enough cash, she rounded a corner and had to slam on the brakes hard to avoid goats on the road. The back wheels went into a skid. A massive tree swam into view and, like a slow-motion horror replay with screeching metallic sound effects, the car grated its length on the trunk before coming to a halt just past it.

Her heart was thumping as if she had run the marathon. Shaken but unhurt, Ophelia jumped out and raced round the bonnet of the car to get a look at the damage. She groaned out loud. Dented and badly scraped, the once glossy paintwork of the passenger side was now a dim memory. She wondered how much the repairs would cost and, in Lysander's immortal words, decided that she didn't *do* regret. At least all the goats were alive to skip around another day and Lysander would stay popular with his neighbours. She had used the art of thinking positively to get through all the worst times in her life, she reminded herself with determination. Why had she lost that habit virtually the same day she had first met Lysander?

She drove on to the village and parked beside the harbour taverna, which had an accommodation sign. A bunch of men were playing backgammon and chatting in the shade of a giant walnut tree. Silence fell when she went up to the bar and requested a room. A waiter noticed the vehicle outside and shouted something. Everyone had to know that it was Lysander's boy-toy car; no doubt the damage had been noticed and they were all making appallingly basic jokes about woman drivers. An outburst of whistles, gasps and comments followed. She could feel her face burning and wished she had abandoned the car on the road. The motherly woman behind the bar asked if she was all right and offered her tea. It was a relief to be shown up to a charming room with a wood floor, a brass bed and pale curtains fluttering in the sea breeze. Feeling overheated in her denim jeans and top, she decided to freshen up in the shower rather than sit and wallow in a misery she refused to acknowledge…

Lysander, who was proud of his absolute control over his temper, saw the yawning space where his Pagani Zonda had been and loosed an anguished groan, raked his fingers through his black hair and almost punched the wall. It was less than three days since he had become a husband, and his wife had left him already. *Left him.* Marriage was much harder work than he had ever imagined it would be. Instead of doing what any normal bunny-boiler would do and cutting up his suits, Ophelia had walked out and he'd watched as she'd driven off in his favourite car. For a male accustomed to constant female pursuit and adulation, such an excess of retaliation was a severe shock. A woman had never left Lysander before, although he had given many women good cause to do so. He was in alien territory. When had a random trace of perfume become proof of extra-marital sex? Why was Ophelia always looking for a way to leave him and escape their marriage? It was bloody insulting! Why had he picked the only woman alive who wasn't happy to live in luxury on a beautiful private island?

He drove two hundred yards down the road and ground to an emergency stop when he saw the tyre tracks across the verge and the black paint slashes on the tree. His stomach lurched inside him. She'd had an accident and nobody had told him! He raked down to the harbour, stopped by the Pagani and leapt out.

The old men below the walnut tree waved and called out cheerful greetings.

'My wife?' Lysander demanded, striding into the bar but already reassured by their manner.

Unimpeded rage roared back through him again in a dam-burst of energising force when he learned that she had taken a room. He took the stairs two at a time and rapped on the door.

After her shower, Ophelia had wrapped herself in a towel and lain down on top of the bed to keep cool. She thought it was the tea she had been promised and opened the door. Dismayed by Lysander's appearance, she fell back a step. 'What are you doing here?'

Even that question was an affront to Lysander in the mood that he was in. He studied her with lacerating force. Her golden hair was tousled, her creamy skin flushed and her ripe curves were covered only by a small pink towel. His view of her full rounded breasts and shapely legs was not one that he would have liked any other man to enjoy. That it bothered him annoyed him, for he had never cared what his lovers wore or how much other men looked at them. He had never been possessive man. Indeed when it came to women easy come, easy go might have been his motto.

'You should've asked who was outside before you unlocked the door,' Lysander told his wife flatly. 'Get dressed.'

Pale blue eyes evasive, Ophelia retreated as far as the bed. 'I'm not coming back, Lysander. We fought all the way to the altar and we've fought continually even during the very small amount of time you've spent with me since we got married. I'm getting on the ferry tomorrow and I'm going home.'

'I will not allow it.'

'No Neanderthal tactics,' Ophelia warned. 'I'm being sensible. Take me to court, bankrupt me, whatever. It won't get you anywhere because I don't want your money, I don't even want my inheritance any more—I just want my life back.'

Lysander dragged in a deep shuddering breath. Her strained eyes and steady intonation telegraphed sincerity and resolve. Her flight wasn't a cry for his attention; she was deadly serious about leaving him. Ferocious tension leapt through his big powerful frame. For the first time in his adult life he felt close to being out of control. Rage was licking round the edges of his every thought like a dark threatening shadow and it unnerved him. He always knew exactly what he was doing, but just at that moment his next potential move was shrouded in mental fog. 'You can have a life with me.'

'I don't want to be rude or start another argument, but life with you is hell.'

Lysander went rigid. Her slightly apologetic tone hit him like an accompanying slap.

A silence that pulsed with undertones hung in the air between them.

Ophelia shot Lysander an anxious glance, her delicate

features tight with apprehension. He realised that she meant every word and was afraid of his reaction. As though he were some kind of domineering bully likely to push her around. *And* possibly lift her up, carry her out to the car wrapped in a sheet and sort out their problems within the privacy of his own four walls. His lean brown hands clenched into fists of restraint lest he prove her right in her suspicions. He didn't like what he was feeling. He didn't like the strange effect she had on him, the bizarre way she infiltrated his thoughts and hijacked his intelligence. He wondered if her emotional excess was contagious and decided to concentrate on basic facts.

'You're actually staging a walkout because you caught a whiff of perfume on my suit?'

Ophelia reddened at the sardonic intonation he employed and straightened her slight shoulders. 'Yes.'

His shout of laughter made her flinch. His brilliant eyes assailed her in blatant challenge. 'Don't you realise that after that interview you gave, I couldn't possibly sleep with another woman without it making headlines? You'll soon find out if I have an affair,' he forecast with derision. 'When you said you were living a fairy tale and I adored you, it was like hurling a challenge at the paparazzi. The media attention will be relentless. They'll watch me day and night when I'm off the island in the hope of catching me cheating on you. Sex scandals sell newspapers.'

Ophelia stared back at him in consternation, for that possibility had not occurred to her. At the same time, however, he was telling her that she had misjudged him, even if he was doing so in a cynical manner that ensured he did not have to actually defend himself or plead innocence. Her head swam a little as she grasped that all-important fact: he *hadn't* been with another woman. Of course, she had already decided to leave him and whether he had been unfaithful or otherwise shouldn't influence that decision. But, for an alarming instant, she couldn't think beyond the fact that he had stayed loyal to her and she could not deny the tide of relief flooding her.

'I didn't think the publicity angle through,' she admitted. 'I suppose I didn't care. I only gave that interview to Pamela's brother to wind you up.'

Lysander studied her with unadulterated incredulity. 'You deliberately set out to annoy me?'

Ophelia evaded his gaze, for, said out loud like that, her plan sounded impossibly childish. 'I thought if I annoyed you or embarrassed you enough, you'd stop insisting I pretend to be your wife and let me go.'

'But in the short term you'd sleep with me, giving every impression of enjoyment?' Lysander slotted in smooth as silk. 'Where does that fit into this scenario?'

Ophelia breathed in so deep she was surprised she didn't inflate, while her complexion turned a similar colour to her towel. 'I don't want to discuss that.'

'Naturally not. But you do acknowledge that you send out very mixed signals? And that talking as though you have just escaped imprisonment and certain death in Bluebeard's castle is rather exaggerated?'

Ophelia tried not to flinch at that scathing comment. She made a desperate effort to change the subject and, with her conscience twanging, opted to be honest with him. 'Look, I don't know how everything's got so horribly complicated—'

'Maybe it's the fact that you argue about everything—'

'Or maybe it's the fact that you just have to be right and have the last word every time—'

'The point *being*?' Lysander prompted drily.

Her eyes flashed. 'I only agreed to marry you in the first place because I thought it would help me find my sister, Molly. I knew I should be sharing any inheritance I got with her. I was planning to use the money from the sale of the house to trace her.'

Lysander was bewildered. 'Your sister? You want to find her? Where is she? I don't understand.'

Ophelia explained to him the story of how she had lost contact with Molly, admitting that she had got her hopes up when the solicitor had mentioned the letter set aside for her wedding day. 'I was convinced it would contain information about Molly.'

'But that letter contained the second will, and the existence of a sister wasn't mentioned in either will.'

'Gran was ashamed of the fact that Molly was illegitimate. There was also a tiny note placed with the second will saying that Molly had been adopted. I think Gran encouraged me to believe there'd be something important in that letter so that I'd marry you. When I realised that my sister had been put up for adoption I felt like I'd run into a brick wall.' Painful tears sprang to Ophelia's eyes and her voice thickened. 'I don't even know what her name is now, or anything about her. How am I supposed to track her down?'

Lysander was disconcerted by her story and his usual cynicism was forestalled by her clear distress. 'I can help you find her. Believe me, there are ways. You should have confided in me before this.'

Ophelia stole a wary glance at him, hope and fear battling inside her. 'Why? All you wanted was the house and you didn't care who you had to walk over or what you had to do to get it on your terms.'

For about five seconds, Lysander met her beautiful ice-blue eyes before she looked away. She looked so sad and that made him feel angry and uncomfortable. His superb bone structure was taut, his stubborn mouth set in a bleak line.

'Confide in you?' Ophelia repeated in an afterthought, resentment stirred to new heights by that unfair reproof. 'Nobody in their right mind would confide in you—you wouldn't be interested.'

'Of course I'm interested in you!' Lysander contradicted in fierce disagreement.

Extreme tension hummed in the atmosphere. She lifted her golden head. 'You're much more interested in business.'

'Have you any idea how many thousands of people depend on me for employment? Of the responsibility I carry in a crisis?'

Her eyes fell from his and she shuffled her bare feet because she was all too conscious of her ignorance. 'No,' she said ruefully.

Lysander surveyed her with mounting fascination. No, she didn't have a clue about the stock-market crisis and only understood or cared when he related it to potential job losses. She had already abandoned a pearl and diamond necklace that was worth a king's ransom, while neglecting to stay married to him for a reasonable length of time would, according to the terms of the pre-nup, lose her a small fortune. Yet she was still prepared to turn her back on any prospect of personal enrichment and leave him. On the ferry. How could she possibly be a gold-digger? No gold-digger would be so hopelessly impractical or uninformed of what was in her own best interests.

'I want you to stay,' he breathed grittily.

Her golden head bent, Ophelia made a tiny awkward

movement with her hands. 'I *can't*. I know it's inconvenient for you if I leave—'

Inconvenient? The use of that word was a positive affront to Lysander because it suggested that their marriage was a trivial matter. His strong jaw clenching, he forced himself to swallow back an angry response.

'Even though I don't understand why and I'm sorry. But I can't live with you—'

'You're bailing out in the first week. How impressive is that? You're my wife…'

'Not really, I'm not—'

'You're my wife. Come back to the house with me, *moraki mou*,' Lysander urged in a roughened undertone.

'What would be the point?' Ophelia was so wound up that her voice ran out of breath on the words.

Lysander swung over to the window in a storm of frustration. What did she want from him? What was he supposed to say or do? What more did she expect? The point was that he wanted her in his bed and that was that. Elaborate declarations were not his style. The seething tension in his broad shoulders spoke for him.

Her attention welded to his lean, powerful frame, Ophelia heard herself say hesitantly, 'I mean…why are you asking me?'

And she was ashamed that she was sinking to the level of voicing that question and backtracking to the point where she betrayed a willingness to reconsider a position she had believed unassailable. Why hadn't she stood firm against his arguments? Giving way to Lysander had already cost her peace of mind, her self-esteem and her values.

Swift to pick up on that potential shift in attitude, Lysander wheeled back round to face her in a movement that was remarkably graceful for a male of his powerful build and size. Stunning metallic eyes glittering, he focused on her with mesmeric force. 'Obviously because I want you.'

'I'm sure you've wanted lots of women,' Ophelia mumbled, slender fingers plucking uneasily at the bedspread, 'but you didn't want any of them for very long.'

Lysander gritted his even white teeth at that unwelcome response, for it was not one with which he could reasonably argue. 'I want a normal marriage.'

Ophelia finally gave him her full attention, glancing up at him with wide astonished eyes, for that assurance was much more ground-breaking than any she had expected to hear. 'A normal marriage? But you spend all your time ignoring me!' she gasped.

'It's only day four…all this is new to me.'

Day four—was it good that he was counting the hours?

'When you say normal…are you still planning on the fourteen-month time limit that you once mentioned?' Ophelia enquired.

'Ordinary marriages don't have a limit. Are you staying?' Razor-edged impatience was slicing through Lysander, narrowing his keen gaze and sharpening the angle of his fabulous cheekbones. He had no interest in discussing the finer details, he simply wanted an answer from her: yes or no.

With very little thought and even less encouragement, Ophelia could have cheerfully asked Lysander another twenty questions at least. Intense curiosity had attacked her. A normal marriage? He had knocked her every expectation flat and startled her with that admission. What had brought about his change of heart? When had he decided he wasn't prepared to let her go? Could he pinpoint the exact moment and what had led to it? What did he find most attractive about her? Least attractive? What made her different from the legions of women who had preceded her? In short, why her and not someone else more beautiful, more accomplished, more his style? Because she wasn't *his* style, was she? She pushed that sudden uneasy reflection to the back of her mind while acknowledging that more questions would exasperate him. For whatever reasons, Lysander had decided that he wanted to retain her as a wife.

'Ophelia…' Lysander prompted in a low growl.

All of a sudden happiness was surging through Ophelia like a river breaking its banks to forge a new course and it frightened her. An ordinary marriage with a guy who was anything but ordinary. He was gorgeous and charismatic and unpredictable. He filled her every thought, influenced her every mood. In the space of three days he had taught her that he was incredible in bed and a world-class disaster as a husband. Cold and distant, he had the power to destroy a vulnerable woman, since there was nothing crueller than indifference. His only passion was sexual, while her emotions ran much deeper. Love had made a victim of her mother and she didn't want to join that club. On the other hand, her late parent had not been married to the object of her affections.

Lysander had moved closer. He brushed long brown fingers through the tangle of glossy blonde hair tumbling over her slight, bare shoulder. Her skin was white and as fine in grain as porcelain against his. The faint evocative aroma of soap clung to her. He found it incredibly sexy. He watched her breathing quicken, her narrow chest rise and fall as she became aware of his touch and proximity. A tremor ran through her reed-slender body. Her long gold-tipped brown lashes concealed her amazing eyes, but the delicate flush of colour on her cheeks told him all he needed to know.

'You are already mine,' Lysander husked with raw satisfaction.

For the first time in several unbearably tense minutes Ophelia allowed herself to look at him. Her defiant gaze locked to his hard, handsome features. 'No…'

'Liar,' Lysander fielded, his dark deep accented drawl making a meal of the contradiction. 'You're on fire for me, *yineka mou*.'

Ophelia snatched in a hunted breath. He had her cornered. The atmosphere sizzled. Oxygen seemed to be in short supply. A hum of erotic awareness was pulsing through her and she was helpless in its hold. His hot, hungry scrutiny held her with spellbinding force. He loosened the towel with assured hands. A slight sound escaped her as the fabric fell at her feet.

'I love looking at you,' Lysander murmured thickly, his attention raking over the sweet curve of her pouting breasts, the quivering tips of her delicate nipples and the pale silky curls that screened her femininity.

His lean, strong face was intent as he lifted her onto the bed and arranged her slim body for his visual pleasure. Excitement and shame engulfed her, but still she couldn't break free. She thought of the bag she had packed, the proud promises she had made to herself, the independent spirit she had believed she could rely on in any crisis. And yet, in the space of a moment, everything had changed because he had made her an offer she hadn't the strength to refuse, even though staying was most probably a mistake. After all, she longed to be loved, while all he required from her was sex…

CHAPTER NINE

LYSANDER studied Ophelia, sensing a lingering tension that went beyond her natural modesty. Her beautiful crystalline eyes still had a wary light that challenged him.

Her heart was banging like a drum inside her ribcage. She reached up and pulled him down to her, wanting his stubborn sensual mouth so much she burned for it. The taste of him was dynamite to her senses. She loved his kiss, the feel of his body against hers. Her fingers delved into his ebony hair and clenched possessively in the springy strands.

He lowered his lips to the swollen crests of her small, full breasts and she loosed a stifled moan. Lying naked while he was still clothed made her feel brazen and yet there was an urgency in her, a newly fierce craving for him that she couldn't restrain. Belatedly she appreciated how much strength it had taken to walk away from him and how overpowering was the sense of reprieve rolling through her in a cathartic surge. With impatient hands she wrenched at his shirt.

'No…' Loosing a husky sound of amusement, Lysander trapped her hands in his and held them captive above her head. 'I like your enthusiasm, but this is my show. I'm about

to drive you out of your mind with pleasure and prove that
business doesn't always come first.'

'You're very confident,' she whispered.

'Always.'

Ophelia connected with his golden bronze eyes and awareness prickled over her entire skin surface, wild anticipation
snaking through her nerve endings. He bent his handsome
dark head to her and she shivered. He kissed her just once;
the slow, deep stroke and delve of his tongue was intensely
erotic. It didn't begin to satisfy her craving, only notched up
her longing a little higher.

He traced a tantalising path of seduction from her delicate
collarbone to the rigid pointed buds of her nipples. A tight ache
stirred in her pelvis and she shifted restively. He took his time,
laving the straining tips of her breasts with his tongue and
grazing them with his thumbs and the edge of his teeth to a
volcanic level of sensitivity that left her biting back tiny moans.

A phone rang. They both jerked into stillness. Lysander
dug his mobile out of his trouser pocket. A slim hand closed
into the front of his shirt. 'No…'

Sleek ebony brows pleating, he stared down at her. 'But—'

'Don't answer it.'

'What is this?'

'Is this a normal marriage?' Her blue eyes were bright as
sapphires, her intonation accusing.

'Didn't I say it was?'

Before he could guess what she intended, Ophelia snatched
the phone out of his hand. Switching it off, she tossed it onto
the dresser and then waited, wide-eyed, for the fallout.

Lysander was stunned by her daring. '*Theos*…' he began.

Ophelia curved slender fingers to his blue-shadowed jaw

line. Metallic-bronze eyes fringed by dense black lashes surveyed her with incredulous force. He was so beautiful, she could hardly breathe for wanting him.

'Kiss me…' she begged.

Lysander almost reached for his phone, just to show her that she could not do what she had just done and expect immunity. But the shy desire in her eyes and the inviting curve of her peach-soft lower lip concentrated his thoughts on more immediate necessities.

'You need to learn my language. *Filise me.*' He translated her request into Greek and waited until she had obediently repeated it. Only then did he respond to her request by crushing her soft mouth under his and kissing her until the blood drummed at an insane rate through her veins.

Desire seemed to punch a hole through Ophelia's lungs and breathing became a challenge as he explored the moist, delicate flesh between her legs. He pushed her hands away when she tried to pull him down to her and pressed his lips to the taut quivering softness of her belly.

'No, you can't,' she mumbled in shock when she realised his objective as he splayed her slim thighs.

Undaunted, Lysander just laughed and called her a little prude, and went right on ahead as if she hadn't spoken. Nothing could have prepared her for that level of intimacy. Intense reaction engulfed her from his first carnal touch. Terrified that the low throaty moans escaping her might be heard beyond the room, she forced her face in a pillow and bit it while her hand closed round the brass bars of the bed and clenched there. Her frantic response pushed her out of control very fast. In an effort to contain the fevered need he had awakened, she dug her slim hips into the mattress. If he

hadn't held her steady she would have writhed. The irresistible charge of sensation forced her quivering, wildly aroused
body to the edge of torment. Excitement surged to an unbear-
able peak and then the sweet melting pleasure consumed her
from inside out. So powerful was that release that it shredded
her awareness of her surroundings for long, timeless moments
of bliss in the aftermath.

Lysander removed his hand from her parted lips and smiled
down at her. 'Noisy little thing,' he teased, long fingers surprisingly gentle on her cheeks, which were damp with tears.
'I love your passion. I love watching you lose control and
knowing that I did it, *hara mou*.'

Her blue eyes open and vulnerable from the lingering
sensual shock of her experience, Ophelia stared up at his lean
dark face and she revelled in his mesmerising smile and
unusual warmth. She felt amazingly close to him. The mortification that had threatened to overpower her at her loss of
control evaporated. So, she had been a little too vocal in her
appreciation and tears had come to her eyes at the height of
ecstasy. In her opinion anything that had the power to make
him look at her like that could not be wrong.

Lysander rolled back off the bed and began to shed his
clothes. 'Tomorrow we will spend all day in bed. No flights
to catch, no interruptions—'

'No phone calls,' she slotted in, lazily enjoying the sight
of the sleek muscled perfection of his strong, hard body. He
skimmed off his boxers revealing the thick jutting length of
his manhood.

'My wife is becoming sexually aware,' Lysander mocked
as he saw her stare and noted the colour unfurling like flags
in her cheeks.

He pulled her into his arms and, watching her steadily, brought her hand down to his bold erection. Now she learned what he liked and it was an exercise that she found wildly arousing as well as informative; the afternoon hours slipped inexorably away and neither of them noticed the passage of time.

Mid-evening, as Ophelia emerged from the bathroom Lysander was on the phone. She was in a bodily daze of satiation, for he had taken her again and again with an insistent passion that had been as exhilarating as it was intense. Now she found that she headed for him with the instinct of a homing pigeon. She leant up against him, driven by an ongoing need for physical contact that was new to her. Disconcerted by that dangerous instinct to stay close to him, she tensed in rejection of the prompting and began to pull away from him again.

Bronze eyes slumberous, Lysander curved a confident arm round her to keep her where she was. 'We're dining at the taverna.'

'The taverna?' she gasped in sudden dismay at the prospect of descending the stairs so many hours after Lysander had come up them. 'Can we just slip out the back way—?'

'Our transport is waiting at the front of the building.'

Ophelia winced. 'I know it's silly but…everybody'll know what we've been doing!'

'We could just have been talking…' Lysander turned to survey the well-used bed with its tossed and crumpled sheets and an unholy masculine grin slashed his handsome mouth. 'Possibly not. But what else do newly married couples do? Why should that embarrass you?'

In fact, when they arrived at the taverna, they were ushered straight out to a private terrace overlooking the beach where they dined by candlelight in perfect privacy. The food was divine and cooked by Lysander's chef, who also owned the taverna. Lysander, when he made the effort and switched off his phone, was incredibly good company. But, try as she might, a certain matter still nudged at Ophelia's newfound contentment and made her uncomfortable.

'I have just one more question about that perfume episode this morning,' Ophelia informed him in a rush. 'No, don't look like that—I mean, I can't help being curious. Does one of your employees wear that perfume?'

Lysander expelled his breath in a long-suffering hiss. 'My mother wears it.'

Ophelia was very much taken aback by that reply for it was the very last answer she had expected. His mother? She felt that it should have occurred to her that he might have family he wanted to see in Athens before he flew out to Kastros.

'Virginia likes to hug,' Lysander added, as if such displays of affection could only be forced on him and tolerated in the name of politeness.

'Didn't your mother want to meet me?' That brash question leapt straight off Ophelia's tongue before she could think better of it. The slight tensing of his strong bone structure warned her that she had the light touch of an elephant in the field of tact.

'She was reluctant to intrude on our honeymoon,' he responded casually.

He was a terrifyingly good dissembler, Ophelia conceded with a sinking heart. He met her gaze levelly, employed just the right note of dispassion and betrayed not an ounce of unease. Yet she wasn't fooled. Somehow—and she genuinely *didn't* know how—she sensed that, clever as he was, he was telling her a whopping fib and most probably doing so out of pity. Evidently his mother—her own mother's former best friend, Virginia—had no wish to meet her son's bride.

Was it an aversion based on Ophelia's parentage? If it was simply the secret wedding that had contrived to cause offence, a few weeks might make all the difference to the older woman's outlook. On the other hand, the alternative—a mother-in-law who totally hated her sight unseen—struck Ophelia as too awful to contemplate. It also reminded her of another necessity she had yet to tackle.

'I've just about wrecked your car,' Ophelia admitted.

'And to manage that within two hundred yards of the garage is pretty good going.' Lysander lounged back in his chair like a sleek black panther ready to pounce. 'You drive like you're on a race track.'

Ophelia went from being anxious and apologetic to stiff and bristling with annoyance. 'No, I do not!'

Lysander planted a strong hand over hers to prevent her from rising from her chair. His brilliant dark gaze was hard, his jaw line squared. 'I watched you leave. You were going too fast for someone in an unfamiliar car. You also drove on after the collision, even though the car was damaged. That was a really dangerous decision.'

'Are you quite finished?' Ophelia prompted tartly.

'*Ne*—yes. Next time you get into a driving seat, you'll be much more careful,' Lysander forecast, lifting her hand and pressing a kiss to her palm in a graceful movement that sharply disconcerted her. 'Naturally I don't want you to get hurt.'

Ophelia swallowed hard. 'You didn't even ask me how the accident happened.'

'Enlighten me.'

Her blue eyes anything but submissive after his criticism, Ophelia lifted her chin. 'I am proud to say that I single-handedly saved the lives of three goats.'

His elegant ebony brows pleated.

'The goats were on the road and it was them or the car,' Ophelia delivered the punchline.

Reluctant amusement lit his metallic eyes. 'Very funny—but you could have been injured and *that* isn't funny, *hara mou*.'

Lysander walked Ophelia out through the bar. Their departure was a slow process, for many of the taverna's diners were eager to speak to him and offer both of them their good wishes. Lysander was held in considerable esteem. He introduced her as his wife as naturally as though he had been doing it for years. His usual formality and reserve were strikingly absent from his manner. It was yet another intriguing glimpse, she registered, of the deeply complex and private man who lay beneath the cold, tough façade that had made him a legend in the business world.

'The worst thing that ever happened to me as a teenager?' Lysander was proud of the reality that he didn't grimace. He wanted his marriage to work and when he put his mind to any objective he was single-minded, thorough and very practical.

'I just feel so close to you when you talk to me.' Ophelia gave him a huge beaming smile that lit up her heart-shaped face like Christmas lights. She was discovering that it took endless digging and encouragement to get Lysander to tell her anything about his past. It was as if he had locked up his entire childhood and thrown away the key of memory.

'The worst thing…' Lysander could not think of one single thing that he wanted to share with her. 'Why don't you go first?'

Two weeks on Kastros with Ophelia had taught him that she liked to talk. She liked to talk…*a lot*, and sometimes she liked to talk about the sort of stuff that Lysander would have happily taken to the grave with him. He had treated other women's conversation as background prattle to which he rarely, if ever, responded. No woman had complained until now, when Ophelia fixed wounded eyes on him and accused him of not being interested in her.

A fast learner, he now knew that if he didn't respond or, even worse, didn't listen, Ophelia would shut up, look unhappy and retreat into herself in a way that he had discovered he absolutely couldn't stand. She wasn't sulking when she did it and she certainly wasn't having a tantrum, but whatever the label he found it intolerable. Disappointment stifled her natural exuberance and made him feel like the sort of guy who kicked puppies. If, however, he gave her the right sort of attention, she glowed and displayed promising signs of turning into the perfect wife. Attentive and sexy, cute and entertaining, very low maintenance, he acknowledged with rich masculine satisfaction. In his opinion, marriage was simply a matter of skilled relationship management.

Clad in a purple polka-dot bikini, Ophelia lay back in the shade, watching the sunlight dance across the glittering surface of the turquoise sea. It was a glorious day. The sundeck on Lysander's magnificent yacht was wonderfully comfortable. She stifled a sigh as she registered that, once again, Lysander had deftly sidestepped her invitation to talk.

'When I went to live with my grandmother, she sent me to a posh co-ed school,' she said ruefully. 'I didn't fit in so I wasn't very popular. I fell for a boy in upper sixth. I was ecstatic when he asked me out. But he dumped me after our first date because I wouldn't have sex with him.'

Recalling his own less than presentable youthful track record in the sexual stakes, Lysander contrived not to wince. 'Boys of that age are a raging bunch of hormones.'

'Yes, well, unfortunately for me, Todd was a liar too,' Ophelia confided heavily. 'He told everyone I'd slept with him. All the girls started calling me a slag.'

'You're very beautiful, *yineka mou*.' Lithe and bronzed and still damp from his swim, Lysander settled down beside her. 'I imagine that you inspired a lot of jealousy.'

'I was badly bullied. When I tried to fight back, the abuse only got worse. That's why I didn't stay on at school to do my A-level exams.'

'I bet the experience made you even stronger.'

'Yes,' she admitted.

Lysander pulled her to him. Arms wrapped round her, he eased her down onto powerful thighs. She responded with an enthusiastic hug and kissed his smooth, muscular shoulder, his strong brown throat and a sculpted cheek-bone in quick succession. His handsome mouth quirked in the sun-warmed tumble of her golden hair. She was very affectionate and it rarely ended in a platonic embrace. He curved appreciative hands to the firm, rounded swell of her bottom and lifted her, clamping her knees to his waist, to carry her indoors.

'Talk first?' Ophelia whispered.

Lysander groaned out loud and brought her into expressive connection with the heat and thrust of the erection moulded by his wet trunks.

Even as she trembled in helpless response, she tipped her

head back. 'Why won't you tell me anything about yourself?' she pressed. 'Why is it such a sensitive subject?'

The suggestion that he might be *sensitive* affected Lysander much like a red rag waved in front of a bull. 'Why would it be sensitive? Perhaps I was trying to protect you from embarrassment. The worst thing that happened to me when I was a teenager?' he repeated in a raw undertone. 'Seeing my father's photo in the newspaper when he was knifed to death in prison! He was a drug dealer.'

Ophelia had frozen in shock in his arms. Aristide Metaxis? A drug dealer? What on earth was he talking about?

'You're the first person I have told about that, so that should please you. It's very exclusive information,' Lysander derided. 'Virginia prefers to believe that I no longer recall being with my birth parents and I've never seen the point of upsetting her by telling her how good my memory of my early years is.'

Ophelia's stunned silence lasted all the way into the opulent saloon. She fixed questioning eyes on his lean hard-boned face. '*Birth* parents? Are you saying that Virginia and Aristide Metaxis adopted you?'

'When I was five years old. My natural mother was a cousin of Aristide's—a minor Metaxis and a drug addict disowned by her family. When she died of an overdose I was four years old and my father tried to use me as a bargaining chip to get money out of her parents. But they didn't want to know and I was left in his charge to be beaten and neglected.'

Ophelia was staring at him in horror. 'I had no idea…I *swear*…I wouldn't have kept on at you if I'd known. I would've minded my own business.' Pale blue eyes swimming, she was in floods of guilty tears, for she finally understood why he was so reluctant to discuss his past.

Startled but surprisingly touched by that emotional response, Lysander lowered her down onto the edge of the pale wood dining table and soothed her with words of Greek. 'Why shouldn't you know? I'm not used to talking about it. I'm grateful that the media never dug up that connection—'

'I had no idea you were adopted.'

Virginia had witnessed Lysander's brutal treatment at the hands of his birth father when Aristide had turned man and child away from their home. Virginia had notified the welfare services and had fought to adopt Lysander. Her actions had undoubtedly saved his life—for his violent father had broken almost every bone in Lysander's body by the time he was five years old. He had required surgery to correct some of the damage.

'I'll never forget what she did for me. Many people tried to dissuade Virginia from taking me on. I was an ignorant little tyke, brought up to shoplift and deliver drugs,' Lysander divulged with a grimace. 'She could have adopted a baby but for some reason she set her heart on me and Aristide let her have her way.'

'Thank God,' Ophelia said fervently, sick inside at the thought of what he must have suffered. 'My mother was never unkind to me and when one of her boyfriends hit her she put him out of the house and wouldn't have him back. She did *try* to be a decent parent.'

Just as Ophelia always tried to be generous, Lysander recognised wryly, wondering how he had ever subscribed to the idea that she was a scheming gold-digger who had known about the second will and who had conspired to deceive him. When he bought her jewellery, she told him how beautiful it was, wore it once to please him, and then put it away in a drawer and promptly forgot about it again. He had never been with a woman like her before. Very much an individual, she defied his expectations and she was always honest in her opinions. There was nothing artificial about her. Yet she also gave him the uneasy feeling that, for all her apparent openness, she still kept part of herself back from him.

In the early hours of the following morning, Ophelia wakened to a familiar pang in her lower stomach that told her that her menstrual cycle was still functioning as efficiently as ever. No, she wasn't pregnant. Well, she hadn't really thought that Lysander's oversight was that likely to result in conception, but even so she couldn't suppress the pang of disappointment that gripped her. She supposed that she should be grateful that she hadn't conceived after Lysander had demonstrated his unmistakable aversion to the idea of fatherhood. Only now she found herself wondering whether she could be entirely happy in a marriage without children. Just as quickly a little inner voice whispered that Lysander would probably not stay with her long enough for it to matter.

She tiptoed out of the bathroom because Lysander was a very light sleeper and she loved watching him while he slept. Shards of dawn light were beginning to slant across the bed, illuminating his male body as he sprawled across the mattress with only a sheet tangled round his lean sun-bronzed hips, a muscular, hair-roughened thigh exposed. The black density of his lashes above his high carved cheekbones was given a tough masculine edge by the blue shadow of stubble obscuring his strong jaw line. His sleek power and masculine perfection were very sexy. She had to clench her fingers to resist the urge to stretch out a hand and touch him. Only when he was unaware of her scrutiny did she allow herself to look at him that way.

She had realised that she loved him that afternoon in the taverna when she hadn't been able to summon up the strength to ask him to leave. But she had no intention of letting her feelings get out of hand as her mother once had. Cathy Stewart had set her heart on Aristide Metaxis and had suffered accordingly. Ophelia was determined not to go down that road, and was equally determined to be realistic. Expecting too much from Lysander would only set her up for a painful disillusionment in the future.

And just how far away *was* that future? Her skin turned clammy. Keeping the ambience light and friendly would suit Lysander much more than anything heavy. She had practically had to torture him just to find out that he was adopted, but at least she now understood the source of his emotional distance and reserve. He didn't trust people. He relied on his own judgement.

Yet the past two weeks had been the happiest of her life, as she loved being with him and treasured the special moments. Top of the list had to be the afternoon when he had apologised for accusing her, or Pamela, for having tipped off the paparazzi about their wedding. Enquiries had revealed the culprit to be an office worker employed by his London legal team. That security leak, on top of the previous oversight concerning the walled garden, had proved one strike too many for Lysander's patience and he had sacked the whole team.

In so many ways, Lysander's attitude towards her had radically changed. She couldn't believe how considerate he was being, how much effort he made to talk to her and ensure that she had a good time. He was much too clever and subtle to leave her with the crude impression that he only wanted her for sex. He had weaned himself off his array of phones and computers and also the business news during the hours that she was awake. She knew he often got up to work while she slept, but that didn't bother her. She was impressed that he was giving her priority over business because he was a workaholic. He really was behaving like a bridegroom on a honeymoon, when she had expected a rather more superficial amount of his attention.

Almost every day they went sailing. He loved the water. He was incredibly energetic and she had been surprised to discover how much she too enjoyed sporting activities. She was learning to dive and waterski and loving the challenge of both pursuits. Her enthusiasm had pleased him almost as much as it surprised him, for he was used to women who were decorative rather than active. Just being with Lysander was exciting.

On the other hand, although he had denied it she was convinced that there had to be a time limit to the duration of his interest in her. He wasn't going to stay with her for ever—she accepted that, of course she did! A normal marriage? What would Lysander know about normal? He led a life of extremes. Extreme wealth, extreme power, extreme privilege. His track record for long-lasting relationships was non-existent. He changed women as other men changed their socks.

Right now, at this very moment, she could only count on one truth: Lysander wanted her in his bed, and when he wanted something—anything—he was used to getting it. Her walkout had genuinely shocked him, but she also suspected that the challenge her departure had presented had increased her desirability by a factor of ten. Once Lysander had accepted that his wealth did not influence her, he had probably just offered her what he guessed would most appeal to her. And that had been a normal marriage, she reflected ruefully. But sooner rather than later, he would get bored.

'I'm not used to seeing you awake this early,' Lysander murmured lazily, breaking into her troubled reverie.

Ophelia jumped and spun round in a defensive movement.

A vision of bronzed magnificence, Lysander pushed his lean muscular length up against the crumpled pillows and frowned at her. 'What's wrong?'

'Nothing's wrong. In fact—' Ophelia pasted a big fake smile on her face '—I've got good news: I'm not pregnant!'

His strong bone structure clenched. 'How do you know you're not?'

'The usual way. I don't need a test to confirm it. So, isn't that a major relief?' Ophelia commented in the same bright voice, while she wondered why he wasn't responding as she had expected.

In fact, Lysander was wondering much the same thing. Perhaps it was her attitude he found offensive, although that was possibly too strong a term. Inappropriate, that was the word he needed, he decided. He didn't like the fact that she should be so delighted that she hadn't conceived his child.

'If you had discovered that you *were* carrying my baby, I would have been pleased about it.'

Astonished by that claim, Ophelia studied him in open disbelief. 'I doubt that. Only a few weeks ago you said you hoped there would be no repercussions—'

'And you're celebrating the fact?' Lysander broke in, his dark, deep drawl harsh in tone as he sprang out of bed.

'Have you got a problem with that?' Ophelia didn't know why he was angry with her and she thought he was being very unfair. She had told him what she thought he wanted to hear and for some peculiar reason she was getting an aggressive response.

'*Yes, I have,*' Lysander said in Greek, hitting the button that opened the doors onto the terrace.

'Say it in English,' Ophelia snapped.

'*Theos*…I don't like your attitude!' Lysander slung at her, throwing her a blistering look of censure from his stunning dark deep-set eyes.

'You didn't want a baby. You don't want to be a father. You made that very clear to me. No woman in her right mind would want to fall pregnant by a guy like you!' Ophelia shouted back at him, tears prickling her eyes, stark bewilderment attacking her as she saw the anger he couldn't hide.

She slammed the bathroom door so hard behind her that even Lysander flinched.

He swore under his breath and paid no heed whatsoever to the spectacular sunrise colouring the early morning sky. He drove long, impatient fingers through his sleep-tousled black hair. He couldn't explain why he felt as he did. She was right: he had never had any desire to become a father. Yet when she had told him she wasn't pregnant, he had experienced a stab of regret rather than relief.

Somehow he had grown accustomed to the possibility that Ophelia might already be carrying his child. It had not seemed so unlikely a result to Lysander. After all, they were both young and healthy. Recent events had made him gradually reassess his reservations about fatherhood.

Yes, his birth father had been a violent man. But why should he worry that he might have inherited that fatal flaw, when he was an adult who had long since proven his ability to control his temper? No doubt if he put his mind to it, he could be a great father. He might have no impressive example to follow in the role, but he certainly knew what *not* to do with a child. He was an intelligent man and adaptable. Life by its very nature was a process of constant change, Lysander reminded himself squarely. His broad shoulders lifted and settled in an easy shrug, his tension slowly ebbing away, until it occurred to him that Ophelia might be less keen on his change of heart.

Ophelia was walking along the beach barefoot when Lysander appeared. The minute she saw him heading down the wooded slope towards her she fell still. Seeing him angry had unnerved her, because cool logic was the very core of his character. Wrenched from her contentment and made to feel insecure, she felt furious, bewildered and scared because she didn't understand why he was so annoyed with her. But none of those emotions prevented her from reacting to his approach with a dry mouth and a fast-beating heart. Casually clad in trousers and a striped silver-and-white shirt that hung loose, Lysander was strikingly handsome.

Lysander saw the anxiety she couldn't hide and an unsettling feeling nibbled down his spine. He didn't recognise what it was and he didn't like it, but he did recognise that it was his responsibility to take care of her and that he did not appear to be doing a very good job.

He shifted shapely hands in a soothing motion that was new to him. 'I got used to the idea that you might be pregnant and I came round to it.'

Ophelia folded defensive arms. She felt as though, once again, she was being wrong-footed by his having switched sides without warning her. She was also furious that she had made the mistake of telling him what she thought he wanted to hear rather than what she truly felt. 'How did that happen?'

Lysander rested metallic-bronze eyes on her. 'I don't know.' A shrug was added for extra emphasis. 'I really don't know. It just happened.'

'But you *must* know! I mean, you were so against it.'

Lysander stared moodily out to sea and shrugged again.

The silence dragged and dragged.

'You know, sometimes I feel like I need to take a tin-opener to you to get words out of you!' she exclaimed in frustration.

'Maybe when…' Lysander ground to a halt, bold chiselled profile clenched hard in the sunlight '…maybe I was concerned that I might take after my birth father and be an inadequate parent.'

Ophelia was so stunned by that amazing admission of potential imperfection and self-doubt that she didn't know what to say. 'Oh…'

'But I only took the time to think about that aspect after I married you. Now I feel confident that I could meet the challenge.' Lysander expelled his breath in a slow hiss. 'Although I don't know how you feel because I never asked you…'

Ophelia hunched her shoulders and studied her feet, bare pink toes digging into the soft sand. She was still in a daze. 'I—'

'I would like a child with you.'

Ophelia blinked once and then again, and then looked up. Lysander was watching her intently and for once in her life she couldn't find words. She was simply bowled over that he should want to have a family with her, for a child struck her as the ultimate commitment. Yet he was a male famed for his aversion to anything that would tie him down. For the first time she honestly believed that her marriage had a proper future and that her husband regarded her as something other than a novelty.

'Me too,' she framed inelegantly, her throat thickening.

His ebony brows pleated. 'But you were delighted that you hadn't conceived—'

'Only because I thought you didn't want a baby.'

His brilliant gaze narrowed. 'It seems that I shouldn't believe everything you tell me, *hara mou.*'

'Cuts both ways,' she fenced. 'You've jumped ship too.'

Lysander hauled her slight body close with enthusiasm. She curved into him as faithfully as his skin. 'Next month I'm throwing a party in London to introduce you to my friends.'

'London?' Unwittingly, her eyes shone like stars. 'So I'll be able to travel from there to Madrigal Court and get back to my garden.'

'You miss it?'

Ophelia gave him a guilty nod. 'It's so beautiful here and the weather is wonderful and I'm happy, really I am, but—'

'You're homesick.' Lysander required no crystal ball to work that out. Listening in on the rather one-sided chats she'd enjoyed with Haddock the parrot on the phone several times a week had proved informative, and she also checked with the horticulturist he had hired on the progress of her garden even more frequently. She seemed to have a personal acquaintance with every single plant she grew. He might have taken her away from Madrigal Court, but her heart and her spirit still lived there.

'Maybe just a little.'

CHAPTER TEN

OPHELIA checked her appearance in the mirror for the tenth time. The tailored green jacket and skirt, teamed with high heels and a fashionable necklace, were the height of formality to a woman who was happiest in jeans. But then she was dressed to impress.

Virginia Metaxis was reputed to be a very chic lady and Ophelia was intimidated by the prospect of meeting her mother-in-law for the first time. Nevertheless, she was also pathetically grateful for the invitation, even if she did suspect that she had Lysander to thank for it. After all, more than six weeks had passed since their wedding. Although his mother had written offering her good wishes for the future, the sheer passage of time had persuaded Ophelia that Virginia was seriously unhappy with her son's choice of wife. The combined history of their families only added to the embarrassment factor. Not only was there the infamous jilting of thirty years ago, but also the long, mortifying saga of Gladys Stewart's bitter determination to be a hostile neighbour to the Metaxis estate steadily expanding on her boundaries.

A limousine ferried Ophelia through the heavy London traffic to Virginia's apartment. For the past three weeks,

Ophelia had travelled between Madrigal Court and the town house almost every day while Lysander generally stayed in the city and caught up with business. An enormous amount of work had already taken place at the Elizabethan manor house, but the restoration was currently entering the phase where important decisions on the décor had to be taken and Ophelia had found her input very much in demand. While she was overjoyed to see the ancient house coming to life again she felt illsuited to the challenge of choosing final finishes and colour schemes. The more conflicting advice she received from the professionals, the more confused and indecisive she became.

Worst of all, the responsibility was eating up time she wanted to spend with Lysander, or working in the garden. But it wouldn't be for ever, Ophelia told herself bracingly. She had discovered that being a Metaxis wife was hard work and her new role had presented her with a steep learning curve. The first week she had feared she might drown in the flood of social invitations and requests for charitable support and visits. She now rejoiced in a personal assistant of her own as a first line of defence. The big party that would formally introduce her to the world as Lysander's wife was only forty-eight hours away. At least she would have met her elusive mother-in-law beforehand, Ophelia conceded wryly as she travelled up in the lift to the older woman's apartment. On cue her mobile phone buzzed.

'Yes, Lysander?' Ophelia answered wearily, for she knew she was being checked up on. 'I'm almost there, beautifully dressed and feeling sociable.'

'There's no need to be nervous.'

'I don't know where you get the idea I'm nervous, and if you're worried that I'm going to put my feet in it by referring to the family skeletons, you can relax,' she assured him in a voice that was slightly shrill. 'All that's done and dusted as far as I'm concerned. I grew up listening to my mother and my grandmother continually rehashing it. Miss Haversham and her wedding dress had nothing on the pair of them, and Aristide's no-show at the church is the last thing I want to discuss with your mother, okay?'

Lysander suppressed a groan. 'Okay.'

'And if she hates me, it's not going to bother me and I'll still be really nice, all right?' Ophelia added hastily.

'Nobody could hate you—'

'Don't talk nonsense,' Ophelia muttered edgily. 'That ex-girlfriend of yours who saw us at the airport looked at me with so much venom, it's a wonder I didn't drop dead on the spot. When I think of how many of your exes are out there—'

'Will you calm down?'

'Lysander…a woman gets *made* nervous by a guy telling them quite unnecessarily to calm down.' On that finishing note, Ophelia dug her mobile back in her bag with a certain amount of satisfaction and walked out of the lift.

'Ophelia…' Virginia was a tall woman with very short grey hair, who looked a good deal older and thinner than she had in the photos Ophelia had seen, but she welcomed Ophelia with considerably more warmth than she'd expected. 'I've been looking forward to this moment for ages,' Virginia explained, 'but I had a treatment plan to complete and it just didn't feel like the right time until now.'

A treatment plan? Ophelia had no idea what her hostess was talking about and wondered if she was referring to illness, or more probably some special course of beauty therapy. But she replied graciously, 'I'm really pleased to be here and I'm

hoping that you will come and visit your old home whenever
you feel like it.'

The older woman's thin features lit up. 'You wouldn't
mind? I must admit that I would love to see the house again,
but I don't like to pry.'

Ophelia hurried to lay that fear to rest and, as Virginia
talked without reserve, she lowered her guard as well. A few
minutes later she was horrified to hear herself say without
thinking, 'Mum always said you were very relaxing to be
around…oh, dear—'

'Please *do* talk about her,' the older woman urged. 'Cathy
was one of my closest friends at school and I very much
regret the way in which our friendship ended.'

'I don't have any feelings of animosity towards you,'
Ophelia hastened to assert.

'None at all? I was surprised that you hadn't told Lysander
that Aristide was involved with your mother for many years,'
Virginia admitted.

Ophelia studied her in astonishment. 'You knew about
their affair?'

'Of course. Three lives got tangled up and spoiled, all
because one man couldn't make his mind up between two
women. And, of course, both those women loved him.'
Virginia gave her a look of wry acceptance. 'I adored Aristide
but he had a weakness for women. I brought him home to
meet my mother at the gate lodge soon after Madrigal Court
was sold to your grandparents. The same evening, Cathy
visited and I didn't exist for Aristide any more. It was love at
first sight for him and I had to be a good sport and accept that
I was only a friend from that point on.'

Ophelia was frowning. She had not been aware that

Aristide had dated Virginia before he met Cathy. It put a different complexion on events.

'Aristide would never tell me why he broke off his engagement to your mother.'

'Are you saying that he finished with Mum *before* their wedding day?' Ophelia could not hide her surprise.

'Two days before. The drama in the church was not of his making and he was appalled when he heard about it. Perhaps Cathy couldn't face telling your grandmother that the wedding was off. Perhaps she believed that Aristide would show up regardless of what he had said. She knew how much he loved her.'

'Yet he married you,' Ophelia countered gently.

'On the rebound. Whatever split them up hurt his pride and he turned to me for consolation. He assured me that it was over between them. Some would say I got what I asked for when I married a man who was in love with another woman. But when you're young, you're an optimist. I thought he'd get over her,' Virginia admitted with a rueful smile. 'He didn't. She was full of fun and very beautiful, and I was always sensible and quiet. It didn't help matters when we discovered that I couldn't give him children.'

'But you adopted Lysander.'

'That was several years later and I'm afraid that Aristide was rather a disinterested father and, of course, Lysander noticed. You have a younger sister, I believe. Does she live with you?'

That sudden change of subject startled Ophelia and she was surprised that the older woman should be aware that she had a sibling. 'Molly? It's more than eight years since I last saw my sister. She was adopted soon after my mother died.'

'Is that so?' A sudden silence fell, in which Virginia seemed oddly uncomfortable and stuck for words. She glanced up with a hint of relief when her housekeeper appeared with a tray. 'Thank you, May. Exactly what we need.'

'Don't get up, madam,' May scolded in an anxious tone. 'You know the doctor said you're to take it easy and get all the rest you can.'

'I'll pour the tea.' Ophelia smiled at her hostess. 'Have you been ill?'

Virginia explained that she had recently completed a course of treatment for breast cancer. Ophelia was shaken by this admission, but did her utmost to conceal her reaction. Virginia was positive about her prospects of making a good recovery, but was equally quick to admit that such calm had evaded her at the outset of the diagnosis.

'Lysander found it very difficult to cope with my illness. He expected the worst and I sensed that, which didn't help me to be brave. He argued with every medical decision and called in third and fourth opinions. However, being Lysander, he couldn't bring himself to discuss his fears with anyone or even admit their existence. He's the strong, silent type and much harder to deal with.'

Ophelia was sinking deeper into shock by the second. From the first moment she had met Lysander, his mother had evidently been suffering a major medical crisis and yet he had not once mentioned the situation to Ophelia or felt the need to share his concerns. She felt terribly hurt. They had been married for more than six weeks and yet still he hadn't got around to telling her. 'Yes, I know,' she said dully.

'I was amazed when he took off and married you without even telling me about it until afterwards,' Virginia continued cheerfully. 'It was so unlike him that I knew it had to be love. When I realised that you'd been nursing your grandmother for months, I insisted that he didn't mention my illness to you. I was determined not to cast a shadow over your honeymoon.'

While Ophelia was relieved by that explanation, she was also stung by the older woman's natural assumption that her son had married for love. The absence of love in her marriage was something that Ophelia tried very hard not to think about, because negative thoughts only made her feel dissatisfied.

'I was starting to fear that Lysander would be single until the day he died and then you came along and I have to tell you—Lysander is transformed,' Virginia declared.

'Transformed?' Ophelia repeated uncertainly.

'Even as a little boy, he was very solemn and serious. He didn't play like other children. When I tried to make him smile he would comply to please me, not because he wanted to. As an adult he never seemed to lighten up. He would tell me that he was happy but all he seemed to do was work—'

'He did a lot of partying too,' Ophelia was moved to point out.

'Yes, but none of those unfortunate women seemed to mean anything to him. I was afraid that my son was rather heartless and now I see that all he was waiting for was—in good old-fashioned parlance—the right woman. Since he found you, Lysander is happy for the first time in his life…'

An awful sense of foreboding was creeping over Ophelia as her mind grappled with what she had found out and put it all together to make a picture. A very disturbing picture that explained things she had struggled to understand weeks earlier. Then she had come up with her own comfortable explanation: that Lysander found her sufficiently desirable to give their marriage a chance, even if he didn't love her.

'How do you know he's happy?' she prompted.

'He's so different. Once or twice he's almost been

chatty,' his mother told her with tender amusement. 'He laughs, he smiles, he tells me little things about you—oh, nothing private, I assure you. He's very loyal. But that bleak wall of distrust he seemed to live behind has been breached. '

As Ophelia focused on the older woman's shining eyes she could feel her heart sinking inside her. If only Virginia's rosy image of their marriage were a true one, she thought painfully. Yet Ophelia could never have understood Lysander's motivation in marrying her without having her first meet his mother or tell her that the older woman had been ill. Every unusual circumstance fitted the scenario Ophelia now saw spread out before her. And the driving force that had kept their marriage afloat against all odds was ludicrously simple and at the same time cruelly cold-blooded: Lysander would have done anything to get his hands on Madrigal Court. Why? Fearing that his mother might die, he had planned to give the house back to her. Whatever the sacrifice, whatever the cost, for Lysander might not be the most demonstrative of sons but he was undeniably a devoted one. She knew what his adoptive mother meant to him. He might even have hoped that the older woman's fond memories of the ancient house would strengthen her desire to survive her illness.

Ophelia finally knew why he had insisted that they would have to pretend their marriage was real if word of its existence became public. To protect his mother. Naturally he would not have wished to distress a sick woman with the news that he had married a stranger purely in an effort to bring her ancestral home back into the family. How could he possibly have admitted that truth to Virginia?

'Are you feeling all right, my dear?'

Ophelia stared back at Virginia and fought the woolly confusion of her racing thoughts. 'I'm fine.'

'You've turned as pale as marble.'

'If I could just freshen up…'

In the smart cloakroom, Ophelia struggled to get a grip on her seething emotions. But she felt as if the ground were tilting beneath her. Her skin was clammy, her stomach unsettled. Shock held her in a crushing embrace of pain. Evidently her personal attractions had not had the slightest influence on Lysander's request for a normal marriage. He was still faking it for his mother's benefit. Virginia was delighted that he was married and Lysander was willing to stay married to please her. And *of course* he was happier now that his mother was recovering from her illness, she thought wretchedly. Health scares did make people much more aware of how much the sick person meant to them.

But where did that leave Ophelia? Madly in love with a guy only tolerating her as a wife out of consideration for his mother. Could she live with that? Have children with him? Pretend that she hadn't put two and two together and added up a total that broke her heart? She hadn't thought that he loved her, but she had come to believe that he found her very attractive and that he cared for her. Only now it seemed that he was simply making the best of a difficult situation.

She crossed her arms and accidentally pressed against her breasts, which had become rather tender. Her tummy still felt slightly queasy. It might just be shock, but she could equally well be suffering the early discomforts of pregnancy. She and Lysander had decided they didn't want to wait. They had seen no good reason to. In a few days she planned to get a test done, but in her heart of hearts she already knew what the result would be. So, it wasn't a matter of deciding what she could live with or without, was it? If she had already conceived, their child deserved a stable background with two parents.

Ophelia rejoined Virginia and managed to talk about Madrigal Court and the party and how much she had enjoyed staying on Kastros. She refused to think a single dangerous thought that might threaten her composure. When she had left the older woman and was able to stop putting on a front she slumped in the lift. She was supposed to be dining out with Lysander. But she couldn't face him. She couldn't face him feeling as she did: cheated, hurt, sorry for herself and angry all at the same time.

Her mobile phone rang. Lysander's name flashed on the screen and she switched it off before telling the chauffeur of her changed itinerary. She would go back to Madrigal Court while she came to terms with what she had found out. A few minutes later, the car phone rang. She knew it would be Lysander and she had to steel herself to answer it.

'I told you Virginia would love you, *yineka mou*,' he drawled with rich satisfaction.

Tears almost blinding her as her eyes flooded without warning, Ophelia cleared her throat. 'I'm not coming back to the town house tonight.'

'Why?' Lysander could hear the wobbly note in her voice and he frowned. 'Are you upset about something?'

'I'm going home. I...I just need a little break from you.'

'Even with good behaviour, you don't get time off,' Lysander said very drily.

'I'm sorry, but I don't want to talk about this.' Ophelia replaced the phone.

What was there to talk about? Lysander specialised in

being brilliant at most things he focused on and, although it went much against the grain to admit it, at that moment Lysander was a runaway success in the husband stakes. He had made her happy. Oh, why stint on the praise? He had made her *ecstatically* happy. He had a knack for doing everything right. It was as if he had come up with a blueprint for a successful marriage and he was following it to the letter.

He made regular phone calls and endeavoured to take an interest in what interested her. If that meant struggling not to shiver in the walled garden in a gale-force wind while striving to demonstrate interest in the flora and enquiring into the meaning of their Latin names, never let it be said that Lysander had shrunk from the challenge. He even managed to put in long hours of work, while giving her the impression that if he had any choice at all he would be with her instead. And when she had confessed that she really would like a baby, the contraception had been ditched there and then. Instant wish fulfilment. What Lysander didn't know about women could be written on a pin-head. He ticked all the boxes in bed—and out of it too. What could she possibly complain about? That he was a caring son? Love wasn't part of their marriage deal. Tears were streaming down her face.

Some hours later, Lysander sprang out of the helicopter at Madrigal Court and strode towards the front door on long, powerful legs. He had cancelled a board meeting last minute. High on rage at his wife's lack of self-discipline and consideration, he strode through the house in search of her.

'Afternoon, Lysander,' Haddock piped up in the Great Hall.

'Good afternoon, Haddock,' Lysander growled, passing by the parrot.

'Metaxis bounder—good-for-nothing swine! You can't trust a Metaxis!'

Lysander froze in his tracks and looked back. Haddock strutted along his perch and broke into a rendition of a nursery rhyme, the living embodiment of an innocent bird. It was pure coincidence, nothing more. The stupid creature had no idea what he was saying. He was merely a clever mimic who repeated phrases he had heard. It would be paranoid to suspect that Haddock was putting the boot in behind Ophelia's back.

The clothing discarded in the master bedroom spoke of Ophelia's recent presence and Lysander breathed a little easier. Her priceless pearl and diamond necklace lay on the dressing table alongside her wedding ring. He fell still, his attention welded to the ring, his wide shapely mouth tightening. There was no sign of luggage, no suggestion that she was packing to go anywhere this time around. Why should she run away? he asked himself angrily. She had no reason to take off again. Why was he even thinking this way?

Ophelia was potting up plants she had divided in one of the newly renovated Edwardian greenhouses. The work had cost a fortune, but the previous poly-tunnels had offended Lysander's aesthetic sensibilities. Her eyes were still overflowing. She sniffed and wiped them irritably on the sleeve of her oversized sweater. She was annoyed that she was being so emotional. She had got the man of her dreams and the baby of her dreams was probably on the way as well. Wasn't there always a serpent in paradise? So, it was a tad demeaning to learn that the man you loved was only making the best of things with you. Well, what had she expected?

Lysander thrust open the door of the greenhouse.

'What are you doing here?' Ophelia spun back to the bench

in haste before he could notice her damp eyes. He looked outrageously out of place in his formal business suit with a striped silk tie and gold cufflinks gleaming at his wrists.

'When you said you wanted a break from me, what did you expect me to do? Just get on with my working day?'

'Yes.'

Feeling the full injustice of that comment, Lysander breathed in slow and deep. 'Did Virginia upset you?'

'She's lovely—and, no, she didn't upset me.' Her golden head was bent as she potted up another plant. 'But realising *why* I'm still your wife came as something of a shock.'

'So, let me into this secret and the shock it dealt you,' Lysander invited.

'Don't be flippant,' Ophelia warned him shakily, scooping up compost and piling it into a pot. 'Let me tell you how it went. Virginia was ill and you were ready to move heaven and earth to buy this house for her. That's why you married me and why you said we had to pretend it was a genuine marriage after the paparazzi reported our wedding. You didn't want her to find out how far you were prepared to go on her behalf.'

'Yes,' Lysander agreed without a shade of hesitance.

Ophelia had hoped he would argue and tell her she had got it all wrong. His agreement of those facts cut her to the quick. The pot she was filling furiously with compost began to resemble a miniature Mount Everest. 'Then you realised that Virginia was delighted that you had married and you decided you might as well hang on to me to keep her happy.'

'No.'

In the tense silence, Ophelia continued to build the compost mountain to a towering height. 'Why are you saying no?'

'I hope I am a good son, but I'm not an idiot. It would be

insane to stay married to a woman I didn't care about. When did you get the impression I was that much of a wimp? Or so unselfish? You're underestimating me, *yineka mou*,' he told her softly.

Ophelia stole a wary glance at him. 'So tell me your side of the story…'

Lysander paced forward and gently turned her round, turning up her wrists and tugging off her gloves. 'My well-laid plans went belly-up around the same day that I decided I had to buy a four-poster bed in which to put you—'

Pale blue eyes perplexed, Ophelia stared at him. 'I beg your pardon?'

'And that was the day after I met you. My reasoning processes were operating on a different frequency from that moment on. I should have stuck to business. You were *supposed* to be a business arrangement.' His lean, darkly handsome features were grave. 'But even though I believed you'd tipped off the paps, I still couldn't wait to get you into bed.'

Ophelia had turned pink.

'I began to make strange decisions. I forgave you for the tabloid interview you did. I decided we had to have a honeymoon. When you walked out on me on Kastros, there was nothing I wouldn't have done to get you back, up to and including cancelling the island's ferry service—'

'Really?' Ophelia was perking up, flattered by that confession. 'Would you have sunk that low?'

'It comes naturally.' Metallic-bronze eyes raked over her heart-shaped face. 'Like loving you.'

'Loving me?' she squeaked half an octave higher. 'Since when?'

'It feels like for ever, *agape mou*. How should I know? I

never felt this way about any woman before, so obviously you were very special from the start. You wrecked my favourite car and what did I do? I *laughed* when you told a bad joke about it!' Lysander curved his hands to her slim hips and lifted her up onto the high stool by the potting bench so that their heights were more on a par. 'We have a great time together. I miss you when you're not with me. I can't wait for you to have my baby.'

It was a declaration of love beyond what she had ever hoped to receive from him. Yet no sooner had she heard it, than she knew she should have realised how much he cared simply by the way he was treating her. The passion had long been blended with warmth, tenderness and respect. Her heart was singing with happiness inside her. 'I guess you're not just with me because your mother likes me—'

'I would just have kept you apart if she hadn't. It would not influence how I feel about you.' Long brown fingers framed her cheekbones and tilted her face up. 'For better or worse, you are my choice and my wife.'

'And totally, madly in love with you,' Ophelia confided unevenly, emotion clogging up her vocal cords. 'I felt so lonely until you came along. That's one of the reasons I was so desperate to find Molly—'

'In another year she'll be eighteen and hopefully she'll decide to look into her past. I'm having enquiries made about her early years with you. It could be helpful to establish who her father is, in case there's a connection. But your details are waiting for Molly on the adoption contact register,' he reminded her as he leant down to her, brilliant eyes intent. 'Now tell me how much you love me.'

There was a hunger in his beautiful eyes that touched

Ophelia and she reached up and kissed him with fierce love and appreciation. 'So much a whole lifetime wouldn't be enough to show you,' she swore passionately. 'Do you really think my sister will get in touch?'

'I believe so, but you may have to be patient.' Lysander smoothed her golden hair back off her brow. 'You should have told me that Aristide had an ongoing affair with Cathy.' As her eyes widened he sighed. 'Virginia thought I should know. No wonder you were so hostile when we first met. Aristide really did work your family over—'

'He got in touch with Mum again when I was a toddler and it wrecked my parents' marriage. He wandered in and out of her life for about ten years. I only saw him a couple of times because they met up in hotels. It was kind of sleazy…'

Lysander pressed a reassuring fingertip to her tremulous lower lip. 'It was love of a kind. Obviously he couldn't stay away. I know the feeling. I can't stay away from you, *agape mou*.'

He bent his handsome dark head and claimed her soft mouth with a ravishing sweetness that left her trembling. They walked hand in hand back to the car and he settled her in and drove off down the lane that led back to the house. She watched him with her heart in her eyes, every fear assuaged, secure in his love and loyalty.

'Oh, yes, there's just one more thing…I *may* be pregnant!' she announced.

Lysander took his attention off the rough surface of the lane to look at her in surprise and pleasure. His charismatic smile lightened his lean dark features.

'We'll know for sure in another few days…oh, no, watch the wall!' Ophelia shrieked as the nearside wing of the big car grazed the stone boundary.

'No goat jokes, *agape mou*,' Lysander warned as he braked to a halt.

But Ophelia was having a hopeless fit of the giggles and although she tried to be tactful and hold them in, she couldn't.

Eighteen months later, Ophelia lifted her daughter out of Lysander's arms.

Shush…, she mouthed in silence, but there was no need to warn him. The entire household knew that Poppy only slept a handful of hours a day and was very demanding in between times. She had her father's live-wire energy—and his adoration. A nanny had joined the staff, but only when Lysander had managed to persuade Ophelia that she didn't need to exhaust herself to prove that she was a good mother.

Weary after a busy afternoon sitting in her buggy watching her mother working in the garden, Poppy snuggled into her cot. She had blonde curls, big dark eyes and an adorable smile, a combination that Ophelia reckoned would someday make her a stunningly attractive young woman. Just now she was a very pretty baby, much admired by everyone and positively worshipped by her grandmother. Lysander was totally enjoying being a father, and Haddock was singing nursery rhymes again.

Ophelia had had a straightforward pregnancy, although she had got fed up with the physical restrictions created by her bulky shape in the later stages. Putting her feet up and resting had proved a severe challenge for someone who preferred to be active. Lysander had gone to great lengths to keep her entertained while Virginia and Pamela had proved wonderfully supportive.

Virginia was maintaining her good health and spent regular

weekends at Madrigal Court. Ophelia had persuaded the older woman to help her with the redecoration and colour schemes for the house and had soon left her in complete charge, for Virginia had great taste and Ophelia much preferred to be outdoors. The once-glorious gardens were in the process of being restored and Ophelia now had a team of gardeners to help her. She got on very well with her mother-in-law. Encouraged by Virginia's simple elegance, Ophelia dressed up a little more often and could now handle all sorts of social occasions without batting an eyelash. At the centre of her assurance was the reassuring knowledge that her husband loved and wanted her no matter what she wore and no matter what she did.

Lysander and Ophelia had only recently returned from a week on Kastros. They walked downstairs and out onto the newly built terrace that overlooked the moat and the glorious gardens. The lush grounds were full of spectacular colour and provided a magnificent setting for the wonderful old house. Pre-dinner drinks were served. Lysander reached for Ophelia's hand. 'I have something I want to tell you and I don't know how you'll take it.'

Ophelia tensed. 'Is it about Molly?'

'No, no further advances in that field, I'm afraid,' he admitted ruefully. 'But what I have to tell you does relate to your family. There is a slight chance that you have another sibling.'

Ophelia held tight to his hand and frowned up at the lean, strong face that she loved so much. 'Another sibling? Are you serious?'

Lysander began to explain. He had been over in New York on business where he'd met the man who was to have been Aristide's best man when he married Ophelia's mother, Cathy. 'In those days, Petros was a close friend of Aristide's and asked him if he knew why they broke up. I wasn't really expecting an answer,' he said wryly, 'but Petros told me that Cathy had admitted to Aristide that she had given birth to a child before she met him and that it had all been hushed up. Aristide was shocked and furious and immediately broke off the engagement.'

'My word…' Ophelia raised her hand to her parted lips, her astonishment unhidden. 'Did you believe him? Do you think it was only a nasty rumour that he heard? Or did he genuinely believe in the story?'

'Petros is no gossip and it was Aristide who told him. Aristide shared only the barest facts: that a little boy was born to your mother at a private hospital and the baby's father took charge of him.'

Ophelia shook her head in wonderment. 'You're saying that I may have an older brother out there somewhere.'

'It's a possibility. Don't get too excited until we have something more solid to go on,' Lysander warned her. 'You're not upset?'

'My goodness, no. It's very sad, though. My mother could only have been a teenager.' Ophelia sighed as they walked back indoors for dinner. 'She really wasn't very good at picking men—'

'But you are,' Lysander cut in, lowering his handsome dark head to claim a long, drugging kiss that reduced her to quivering compliance in his arms. 'You picked me, *agape mou*.'

Her crystalline eyes danced. 'Only because you were willing to pay the water charges. But you didn't accept the cash I offered you.'

Much amused, Lysander grinned down at her in the Great Hall. 'No, and then you used the money for something else!'

'Did I?' Ophelia was very much disconcerted by that information. 'Oh, that's right—I gave the money I owed you to the vicar for the church roof fund.'

'It was still the best investment I ever made, Mrs Metaxis.'

'Lysander's my hero!' Haddock carolled on cue from the corner, carefully coached as he had been to react to the name Metaxis with what Ophelia deemed to be a more socially acceptable response.

Unfortunately, Lysander had proved less impressed than she had hoped.

'Well, you *are* my hero,' Ophelia pointed out, leaning against her husband and gazing up at him from below her lashes with a look of unashamed admiration and contentment. 'I love you very much.'

A meeting under the mistletoe

SHERRYL WOODS • HOLLY JACOBS
DARLENE GARDNER

*A meeting under
the mistletoe*

*Christmas
Eve Kisses*

Amy's gift-wrapped cop...
Merry's holiday surprise...
The true **Joy** of the season...

*For these three special women,
Christmas will bring unexpected gifts!*

Available 5th December 2008

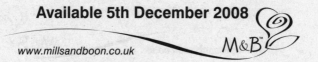

www.millsandboon.co.uk

M&B

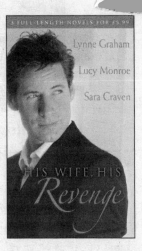

Celebrate 100 years of pure reading pleasure with Mills & Boon®

To mark our centenary, each month we're publishing a special 100th Birthday Edition. These celebratory editions are packed with extra features and include a FREE bonus story.

Plus, you have the chance to enter a fabulous monthly prize draw. See 100th Birthday Edition books for details.

Now that's worth celebrating!

September 2008

Crazy about her Spanish Boss by Rebecca Winters
Includes FREE bonus story
Rafael's Convenient Proposal

November 2008

**The Rancher's Christmas Baby
by Cathy Gillen Thacker**
Includes FREE bonus story *Baby's First Christmas*

December 2008

One Magical Christmas by Carol Marinelli
Includes FREE bonus story *Emergency at Bayside*

Look for Mills & Boon® 100th Birthday Editions at your favourite bookseller or visit
www.millsandboon.co.uk

FREE!
4 Books
and a surprise gift!

We would like to take this opportunity to thank you for reading this Mills & Boon® book by offering you the chance to take FOUR more specially selected titles from the Modern™ series absolutely FREE! We're also making this offer to introduce you to the benefits of the Mills & Boon® Book Club™—

- ★ **FREE home delivery**
- ★ **FREE gifts and competitions**
- ★ **FREE monthly Newsletter**
- ★ **Exclusive Mills & Boon Book Club offers**
- ★ **Books available before they're in the shops**

Accepting these FREE books and gift places you under no obligation to buy, you may cancel at any time, even after receiving your free shipment. Simply complete your details below and return the entire page to the address below. You don't even need a stamp!

YES! Please send me 4 free Modern books and a surprise gift. I understand that unless you hear from me, I will receive 6 superb new titles every month for just £2.99 each, postage and packing free. I am under no obligation to purchase any books and may cancel my subscription at any time. The free books and gift will be mine to keep in any case.

P8ZEF

Ms/Mrs/Miss/Mr ....Initials ....
Surname ....
Address.. **BLOCK CAPITALS PLEASE**

....
....Postcode ....

Send this whole page to:
UK: FREEPOST CN81, Croydon, CR9 3WZ